John 3:30

RAISEN'

by Hoke Shirley

Hoke Shirley

LAUREL
Mountain
PRESS
www.laurelmountainpress.com

Table of Contents

Copyright © 2008 by Hoke Shirley

ISBN 978-0-9799834-1-2
Library of Congress cataloging in progress.

Cover photo by Hoke Shirley
Back cover photos by Hoke Shirley and Tracy McCoy
Cover design and layout by Terri Johnson
Edited by John Shivers
Published by the Laurel Mountain Press -
P.O. Box 1973 Clayton, Georgia

Printed in the United States of America

IN DEDICATION

*To my Lord and Savior Jesus Christ whose
great intervention and redemption in my life
are now characterized by the fact that I am alive
and able to serve Him.*

*To my dad Sam Shirley, the great storyteller,
who's unforgettable tales are brought to life in
this series of books.*

*To my wife Jackie whose smiles, as I wrote,
encouraged me greatly.*

*To Stacy, Celena, Kinley, Kaplan,
Kaden and Kasen
Kyle, Regina, Montgomery and Madison
Nathan and Vanessa – who were all excited
that dad – pops – pawpaw was writing a book.
This kept me excited.*

*To Terri Johnson, Steve Townsend,
Rob Murray, Jordon Poss,
Mary Elizabeth Law,
Hoyt Speed and Reed Mashburn,
thanks for all of your help.*

*To Georgia Power Company where the
professionalism and compassion of their
people, from top to bottom
(many of whom I call friends)
is unmatched in the business world.*

*And to all of the wonderful people, that I call
family and friends, who make my home,
Rabun County, so special.*

Proverbs 22:6

"Train up a child in the way he should go: and when he is old, he will not depart from it."

Mountain Paraphrase:

"If ye give yer young'uns a good Raisen' ye won't lose em' when they grow up."

CHAPTER 1 SLEWFOOT

As always, late spring in Rabun County was glorious, with the new growth of leaves on the trees looking so fresh and beautiful, and the mountain laurel blooming. The morning air was clear and still cool from the night before. Leed Brown, a slim, muscular, handsome, dark headed, mountain boy of 17 was out early logging with his dad, Telford Brown, a strong, and dark to graying haired former WW II Sergeant. With them was his brother, Benji, a 16 year-old who took after his mother's side of the family and was thus blonde, round faced and stout built.

As Leed waited for the mule to drag the next log into the yard, he looked up to the steep ridge that led down from Crumley Mountain. He thought he saw something moving down the spine of the ridge along the government line. He studied intently for a minute but couldn't make out any further movement. Could have been a revenuer, he thought. With all of the liquor made in these woods they were always looking. Or maybe it was a varmint heading down to the farm. If so, it would have to deal with Grandpa Brown who didn't allow any chicken thieving on his watch.

Then the mule came into the yard and Leed turned and with two swings of the sledge hammer in his hands, he knocked the J-grabs out of the log. He slapped Ben, the mule, on the rump and told him to get back up the hollow to where his dad and brother were. They had cut and limbed the logs the day before, and Leed's dad and brother were sending them down to the yard. They would load them later that morning.

As he moved down the ridge from Crumley Mountain, he saw the dark headed boy standing down in the log yard, so he stopped to keep from being noticed. As the boy stared his way, he looked back, knowing that the two bushy white pines he was standing behind kept him hid, while the small opening between them allowed him a good view. He stood perfectly still, so as not to jeopardize his mission. Finally the boy turned, as the mule entered the yard, and he continued pushing carefully through the undergrowth on his descent to the farm below.

In the old house at the farm, Leed's grandparents, Jeremiah and Ruby Brown, were going about breakfast. Since they were in their early seventies, they didn't hit it as early as they used to and were having a late breakfast. As Ruby fried eggs and sausage on the wood cook stove, Jeremiah sat at the table and sipped black coffee. Ruby asked, "What'cha gonna' do today?" and Jeremiah answered, "I thank I'll walk up to the upper field and see how growed up it is, I might have to mow it soon. I believe I'll take that old dog with me too. Might get that sorry thang to run somethin' instead of layin' around on the porch all the time."

Jeremiah and Ruby were totally unaware that an intruder, with larceny on his mind, was descending down from Crumley Mountain as they talked.

He was now at the edge of the woods, at the farm, looking out. When he felt that his presence had not been detected, he eased out and walked quietly up to the hog lot. As he peered in through the slats of the fence, Sadie the sow was rooting and didn't notice him standing there. Suddenly she sensed something was wrong and looked abruptly into his dark eyes. Fear tore through her and then

3

she let out a squeal! With the warning, everything in the barnyard went crazy, running, squealing, snorting and flying as he crossed over the side of the hog lot and quickly grabbed a pig. In the excitement he headed the wrong way, climbing over the front of the lot, running with the squealing pig right across in front of the farm house.

The second Jeremiah heard Sadie squeal he leapt to his feet and ran toward the bedroom, and reached up for Old Betsy, his 50 caliber muzzle loading rifle that hung over the door. As he turned toward the front door, he glimpsed something outside the window, behind the couch. "Thar goes Slewfoot, the bear with a pig in his mouth!" Jeremiah exclaimed as he dropped to one knee on the couch and poked the gun right through a widow pane, just above the back of the couch, as he pulled back the hammer. He took quick aim at the gigantic fleeing bear and pulled the trigger. Smoke billowed so that he couldn't see out the window. He quickly rose and went to the front door as Ruby asked, "Whygged knock out the window fer?"

As Jeremiah came out on the porch and looked out in front of the house where he had last seen Slewfoot, he frowned and asked, "Where's that sorry dog? If he'd been don'in his job, that bear wouldn't be runnin' off with no pig in his mouth." The sorry dog was standing around the side of the house and when he heard his name, he dropped his head, pulled his tail between his legs, and slinked up under the house to make himself scarce.

Jeremiah quickly stepped off the porch and headed out through the dissipating smoke where he saw a scared but only slightly roughed up pig that Slewfoot had dropped in the commotion, running back to his mom. Far off to his right he saw Slewfoot crossing a lower field at high speed, taking thirty-foot a jump, leaving the country. He looked all around but found no blood and knew that he had missed that thieving bear again.

At the report of the rifle, Leed said to his dad and brother, who had gathered at the yard to start loading the logs, "Grandpa's shoot'n at old Slewfoot again," and they all laughed, knowing that Grandpa thought himself a great hunter and an excellent shot, but fell way short when it come to dealing with this wily old bear.

After they finished loading the log truck, Telford told the boys to send the mule home. They laid the traces across his back and wrapped them around the hames where the reins were already bundled tightly. When finished, Benji slapped the mule on the rump and told him to go home. It was a short trip down the road that split the property that Jeremiah had given to Telford and his brother Latimer.

As Telford drove the 1938 F8 Ford, with the dead tandem down the road they came to the big mud hole that was still full of water from the rain that fell earlier in the week. He looked at the boys and said, "I don't know if we'll make it through with a big load like this." He took a deep breath, let out the clutch in granny gear and crept forward until the front tires entered the mud hole. Then he gunned it. The truck did well 'til it reached the far end of the mud hole, where it bogged out and started spinning on the left side.

Telford and the boys got out on the running board and jumped to firm ground that ran along both sides of the mud hole. After the boys had walked from the right side to the front to meet their dad at the end of the mud hole, they all just stood and studied the situation. Finally Benji said, "Dad, can we hook the long log chain in the slot of one rim between the dual wheels in the back and then out to a tree, and use the rear wheels like a big winch to drag the truck out like you showed us one time?" His dad answered, "No son, there ain't no tree big enough and close enough to hook to."

As they pondered, suddenly Leed got that look in his eye as he always did when his brain was in high gear. He walked quickly down by the driver's side door and studied the front set of rear dual wheels, which were the drive wheels. Then he turned to his dad, who had followed him and was studying his son with an interesting look on his face.

"Dad, do you remember when we helped ye put the dead tandem under this truck?" Telford said, "Yes." His interesting look was intensifying. Leed asked, "Do ye remember you showed us how a differential worked when we gutted the third member?" Again Telford said, "Yes."

"Well, the way I see it is, if we hook the chain between the rims on the side where the tires are spinning, like we would if we were going to use it like a winch. Then hook the chain up around the big crossbeams on the truck, when the chain gets tight these tires won't be able to spin. That'll make the differential send all the power to the tires on the other side that have traction on firmer ground."

5

Telford looked at him with a smile and said, "Son, I think it'll work; let's give it a try".

His time spent as a sergeant in World War II let him know that this was a good time to build confidence in his two sons, so he said, "Benji, you drive and Leed, you run the show and tell us what to do." As Benji climbed into the cab, Leed and his dad pulled out a long log chain and hooked it in a slot of one rim between the dual drive wheels. Then they hooked the other end around the crossbeam of the bed just in front of and above the tires. Leed and his dad backed up a little, and then Leed looked at Benji and said, "You'll have to feather the clutch until you take up all the slack in the chain. If you dump the clutch and start the tires spinning hard, when all the slack is taken up in the chain, the inertia will jerk the load down and side ways so hard that it'll turn the truck over, since it's already leaning this way." So Benji eased out on the clutch several times until all the slack was taken up, then he applied enough power to turn the other wheels that had the traction so that they slid the tires that were locked by the chain. The younger boy kept the engine at a steady pace until the tires on the passenger side started spinning, just as the truck was almost out of the mud hole.

At this point Leed hollered at him to stop and to back up just enough to release the tension on the chain so he could unhook it. Benji did, and after unhooking the chain, Leed told him to pull up out of the mud-hole about 100 feet, stop and then back up slow to unwind the muddy log chain from around the dual wheels.

After the operation was complete, Telford silently praised the Lord for the blessing of these two fine sons, as Benji drove the truck and they all rode up to Ritter's saw mill, across the railroad track, above Mountain City, to sell the logs and unload them in the big storage yard by the band mill.

On their way back home, they saw Loge Rodgers walking, in his normal manner: long steps and swinging arms, as he made his way up the road in his overalls. Telford said, "Boys, if you wave at Loge he'll wave back every time, but if you don't wave, he won't never wave a'tall." As they drew near to the lone walker, Leed threw his hand up and Loge gave a quick straight up and down wave back with his right hand but his face remained straight forward, and they never caught his gaze behind smoked colored round glasses. The boys were struck with this sight of a man who didn't look sideways, but saw sideways anyway, so they grinned and looked at each other.

As they neared home, Leed asked his dad, "Since School's out now and we're working all week with you, can we have this Saturday off?" Telford answered, "Sure, if we can have a load of logs ready Friday evening, I can take 'em to the mill on Saturday by myself, then take the rest of the day off and take your mom to town." Leed continued, "Can we drive your pickup over to Lake Rabun that afternoon after it gets real warm?" Again Telford said, "Sure, just be careful."

———————————————

Next Saturday morning the boys, feeling the freedom that comes with a day off from work and with school being out, got up early and came into the kitchen where their mom, Linda Brown, an attractive blonde who definitely did not show her age, already had breakfast ready. "Morning boys," she called out cheerfully. Linda went over and turned off the radio as a Hank Williams song ended. As they sat down their dad said, "Boys, we was about to start without ye, now let's bow our heads, 'Father we thank You for Your continued blessings and I ask that You would protect Larry and Ronald over in Korea. Father, keep Your hedge of protection around them as they are serving their country in harm's way. Also, bless this food for the nourishment of our bodies. I ask these things in the name of Jesus Christ my Lord and Savior, Amen'." Larry and Ronald, Leed and Benji's two older brothers, were both serving in Korea. One was in the Army and the other in the Marines.

After breakfast Telford got up and headed for the door to take the load of logs to the mill. Telford looked at them, grinned and said, "Have a good time today but be careful." "OK," The boys answered in unison.

After Telford left, the boys walked up on the big ridge and swung on the ropes they had placed in some trees in the hollow, then they walked on over the mountain to swing on the ropes over the cliff that was part of the way down the back side of the mountain toward the river. They had thought of this after seeing a Tarzan movie a few weeks earlier. The cliff was pretty high, so the ropes

7

that were tied up over the cliff had several knots in them to hold on to when they were swinging and doing the Tarzan call. They knew if their mom saw them swinging out over the cliff she would make them stop, so they were quiet about the Tarzan stuff. They tired of this after a couple of hours and headed back over the mountain and down the ridge toward the house. As they walked, Benji started singing, "I got a rabbit in the log and I ain't got my dog", then Leed smiled and joined in singing the old hobo song.

At home they checked in with their mom and then got in their dad's beautiful, red 1941 Ford pickup to go to Lake Rabun. As Leed opened the door, stepped up on the running board and slid onto the seat of the truck, he admired the large steering wheel and the long slim double crooked gear stick that stuck up out of the three speed transmission in the floor. He knew why his dad liked this truck so much and made sure the truck was washed every time it got dirty. He even changed the oil once a month.

As they pulled out of the yard and headed down toward the highway, their conversation was about how warm it had been, and that the water would probably be warm enough to swim in today. They both had their cut off jeans lying on the seat between them.

As they talked, while the highway passed beneath them, they failed to notice Loge Rodgers walking up the road in their direction. Benji finally saw him at the last minute and threw up his hand just as they were almost beside him. To their absolute amazement Loge immediately gave his characteristic and pronounced up and down wave, but he never altered his gaze from straight forward. Benji said, "That's amazing, he can see out the side of his head." And Leed answered, "No I've read about this; he has peripheral vision, which means he can see sideways out of his eyes as well as forwards." "Wow that would be neat." Benji said, the amazement evident in his voice.

As they drove up Lake Rabun Road through the tight curves, between the rock walls and by the big houses, they remarked how pretty it was, and about how they hoped some girls would be around the lake today.

Their first stop was the boat ramp, fueling and dock area which, second only to the U.S. Forest Service campground and beach at the headwaters, was the most popular place on the lake. They parked across the road to give plenty of room for folks to put their boats in, and walked down the wooden steps to the edge of the dock, where the gas pumps that filled the boats with fuel were located.

A new 1953 Buick Wagon was getting ready to back a beautiful, wooden, Chris Craft on a trailer into the lake to unload. For a minute the boys just stared at the beautiful wood grain of the high-priced Chris Craft and how the chrome on the equally high-priced Buick shined. Then they walked over from the pumps to the ramp to ask the gentleman in the Buick if he needed help putting the boat in.

After they asked, he answered "No, my daughter is going to ride it into the lake and pull it over to the dock." About that time the most beautiful blonde girl that Leed and Benji had ever seen walked around the front of the Buick and said, "Hello." Both boys stood with their mouths open before each finally got out a, "Hey!"

After the boat was launched and while the attendant was filling it with gas, the gentleman introduced himself as Daniel Thurmond and his daughter as Danielle, from Atlanta. Then he asked, "My daughter wants to ski today, but I don't have time to drive the boat for her since I have to review some documents this afternoon. If you don't mind, would you boys go skiing with her this afternoon? Then come with her around to the Stone Place to dock the boat, and I'll bring you back to your vehicle." Benji bluntly asked, "You live at the Stone Place?" The gentleman smiled and said, "Yes, when we're in the mountains. Also there are new skis in the boat, so I think you will enjoy this afternoon." Both brothers said in unison, "Yes sir."

Danielle and the boys all got their swim gear on in the bathrooms in the store that was part of the dock, and came back out and hit the lake. Benji asked, "Can I ski first?" Danielle agreed, and Leed volunteered to drive the boat. After they had navigated their way through the idle zone at the dock, they stopped at the edge of the main part of the lake so Benji could rig up.

The boys had skied once and had also ridden an aquaplane the summer before, with a friend of their dad's from Clayton who owned a boat, so they knew what to do. In fact, Benji was an excellent skier thanks to his strength and balance. On the first try he was up and they headed up the lake planning to go through the narrows and turn around in the big basin so Danielle could ski back. With

9

the powerful boat they leveled out quickly and headed up lake. Leed was staying in the middle of the waterway, but Lake Rabun was so crooked, as it weaved its way up between the mountains on each side, that he was giving Benji a pretty good ride at the end of the rope. The Chris Craft had a lot more power than the boat that had pulled Leed and Benji the summer before, and Benji was really enjoying the extra speed.

But again and again, as they went up the lake and on into the narrows, Leed's eyes were drawn to Danielle and the beautiful bathing suit she was wearing. Her skin was smooth, and beautiful, and already tan, and it wasn't even summer yet. He noticed as she smiled that her teeth were as white as an egg shell and all of them were straight. Leed was bashful and had never had a girlfriend at school, even though he thought about girls a lot. As he kept looking at Danielle, while she looked back at Benji, who was doing some fancy skiing on the new skis, he noticed that his breath was getting short and his palms were sweating on the steering wheel.

As always in these situations, his mind, which normally thought through each situation quickly, was running wild to the point that he couldn't even think at all. As he gulped to get air he was brought back to reality by a yell from Danielle, "Look out you're headed for that point!" Leed was startled and almost froze, before finally jerking the steering wheel hard left so as to just barely avoid the shallow water and the wave exposed red clay that was the small point. Benji didn't have the option to dodge, he started to drop into the water but the quick maneuver of the boat accelerated him so much that he felt he would skip across the water and hit the red clay incline and get hurt. He made a quick decision bolstered by his daring to ride it out, so he held onto the handle of the ski rope and crouched ready for the jump. With the new skis and the slick wet red clay, the point made a fair jump platform and Benji got some good altitude, but tipped a little and fell as he landed with a big splash.

He was whooping and laughing, when a very embarrassed Leed and a stern looking Danielle idled up to get him. Once he was in the boat and through talking about how fun that had been, Danielle asked him to drive while she skied on in to the big basin and then back to The Stone Place.

Danielle was a great skier and put on a show as they passed

the other slower boats that were mostly still pulling people on the long, wide surf board looking aquaplanes. The slower, older boats couldn't go fast enough to pull a skier so they relied on the aquaplanes which would float a rider at a very slow speed and were easy to stay up on.

After they arrived at The Stone Place, Daniel Thurmond met them at the dock and asked Danielle if they had a good time. As Leed held his breath she said, "Yes, daddy." He thanked the boys and said, "Come with me." After they entered a storage area adjacent to the dock Mr. Thurmond said, "Would you boys like to have these old skis? I'm going to throw them away since I have the new ones now." The boys looked at the three pairs of skis which were in good shape and answered, "Yes sir." He then offered to take them back to their vehicle but Leed said, "No, it's not far. We'll leave the skis up at the road, walk over to the truck and then pick the skis up on the way by." Mr. Thurmond thanked them again for spending the afternoon with his daughter. Leed and Benji told them both bye and headed back to the dock.

After the boys got the truck, picked up the skis, and were heading home, Benji asked Leed what he was going to do with the skis they had just gotten. Leed said, "I don't know but I'll think of something."

2 STONEWALL FALLS

On Monday a man named Martin came over and cut hay in two of the big fields where Telford and Jeremiah didn't let cows graze, so they could have feed for the winter. Leed liked to watch the mower lay down the tall grass as it circled, and circled again and again.

With the sun out, the hay was ready to bale on Wednesday, so Martin brought his hay-rake back and windrowed the hay. Then he brought over his New Holland 66 hay baler. It would pick up hay in the front and spit square bales out the back, knotting the string around the bales automatically. What a sight to see.

Leed couldn't watch this wonder long because they had to load the bales onto Telford's and Jeremiah's trucks and get them into the two barns. This was hot, hard work that required a stop by the well to drink a dipper full of water, each and ever trip. That evening, when their mom was leaving for church they were still hauling.

The hay made them itch so when they finally finished, the two tired boys asked their dad if they could go to Stonewall Falls and take a bath. He said, "Sure boys, but ye better hurry, the sun's getting on over."

They ran to the house, changed into cut off jeans, grabbed a bar of Ivory soap, a couple of old tattered towels and took off. When they got there the breeze that always came off the falls was really cool, as it usually was in late evening. They dropped their towels on the rocks near the edge and waded through the pool over to the ledge on the right. It was necessary to ease along the rock ledge in a crouch, because the mist from the falls kept the stone wet and slick. From their experience wading and fishing, they knew where water runs over rock it usually ain't slick, but where just mist lands on rock, it can get really slippery.

They came right over to where the falls pour down on the throne and spill out into a small pool on the ledge, before dropping finally into the big pool. They took turns doing pushups down in the small pool to get wet, which elicited a few, "Wow, that's cold," yells as the frigid water almost took their breath. They took turns lathering up and then came the fun part, sitting on the throne.

The falls concentrated a little bit on the East side and poured down a slight vee. At the bottom of that vee was a small flat ledge, about chest high, above where they were lathering up. The numbing effects of the cold water required that they take turns slipping up the rocks and backing in and sitting down on the small ledge. About half of the creek poured down on that ledge all the time, and when Leed or Benji sat on what they called the throne, the cold, pounding water would just beat their heads, shoulders and backs. This was a very rough, but after a hard day a haying, it made for an enjoyable massage. When they were through and heading back to the house their bodies were cool and still tingling from the cold water rub-down.

The following Thursday the boys went to town with their dad to get some auto parts at Jones Auto Parts. While their dad was inside they stayed outside to look over at the courthouse and the jail across the street. "Look," Benji exclaimed, "that's a new Chevrolet parked over there." He gestured towards the courthouse, "Let's go see it."

The boys walked across the street and when they got close, Benji remarked, "I ain't never seen no car that was yeller and green before, but it shore is pretty!" "That color combination is called 'Cream and Green'." Leed informed him, "I heard dad talking about how pretty it was. I bet this was the car he was talking about." Benji wondered aloud, "Yeah, I guess it belongs to some rich feller that works in there in the court house and has a good payin' job. I guess the only job we can get, when we get out of school is logging, or a public job maybe with Reeves or Ritter's or the Forest Service. Or maybe we just join the army like Larry or the Marines like Ronald." Leed injected, "Maybe we can get a job with Georgia Power Company?" Benji turned his head, smiled and said, "Boy, that would be great!" They headed back across the street to their dad's truck.

While they were standing next to their dad's truck, they saw a brand new truck coming from town. As it drew nearer, it slowed and pulled over to where they were and stopped. As it pulled in, they realized it was Mr. Jordan Laycock, the local Georgia Power Resident Engineer, who had gotten to know Telford and the boys and had taken quite a liking to Leed. Mr. Laycock said, "Hello." But the boys just stared at his new truck with their mouths open, until finally Benji asked, as he looked intently at the emblem on the side of the hood, "What is a GMC Hydramatic?" Mr. Laycock said, "This pickup truck has a four speed, automatic shift transmission, which is new this year from GMC and it's the first time ever offered in any pickup." He said, "Look at the shifter," and the boys looked in the window of the cab at a gear shifter on the column, that looked like a regular column shift on a truck. It was hooked to a readout that stuck up on the steering column that read, [1-4 1-3 1-2 R]. Mr. Laycock explained that when you put the shifter in R and cut off the switch, that reverse becomes park and the truck would not roll.

The boys were still oohing and awing at the truck when Mr. Laycock asked how their school year had gone. Both brothers said fine and then Mr. Laycock looked at Leed and asked, "How about your study in those engineering books that I loaned you. How's it going?" Leed answered, "Good. I'm starting to understand more and more, and that makes it very interesting." "Good," Mr. Laycock replied, "maybe you can get into Georgia Tech." "That would be great," Leed agreed.

Then Benji spoke up and asked, "Mr. Laycock do you want him to get above his raisen'?" The Georgia Power engineer wisely returned, "Hopefully your raisen' will prepare you to do well in life, wherever you go and in whatever you do." Benji with an enlightened gaze answered, "Well I never thought of it that way." Mr. Laycock invited Leed to come to his house some time, so they would review the material in those engineering books he had been studying, to see if he had any questions or needed help with the formulae. They exchanged goodbyes and Mr. Laycock drove off with the boys watching as the Hydramatic transmission carried the power from the quiet motor quickly and smoothly to the 6.00 x 16 rear tires as he went around the curve and down by the high school.

When he got out of sight Benji asked, "How does an automatic shift transmission work? In fact, how does a regular transmission work? How do they get the power from the motor to the tires?"

Leed answered, "Well I've been a readin' about that and what happens is they both have gears with different speed ratios inside to give different output speeds, depending on what gear they're in."

"What's ratios?" asked Benji.

Leed looked at him, smiled indulgently and said, "Well the motor is turning at a certain speed depending on where your foot is on the pedal, so the fluid coupling on the hydramatic transmission sends the power to the planetary gears, where it changes the speed and sends it to the rear wheels."

Benji looked kinda lost. "What's a fluid coupling?" he asked. Leed still patient, answered, "That's the thang that catches the power from the motor shaft and converts it to hydraulic power to run the hydramatic transmission. Now, in a manual transmission like dad's truck has, the motor turns a flywheel and when you let the clutch out the friction of the clutch grabs the flywheel."

"What's friction? They talked about it in school, but I still ain't got it figured out." Benji confessed. Leed, feeling like this might be a lost cause, was saved by his dad coming out of the parts store. He wanted his brother to understand, so he said, "I'll just have to show you that one!" On the way home Leed thought and thought of how he might show Benji what friction was; then it came to him. He would just show him what happens when you take friction away.

When they got home their dad went to work on the big F8 Ford. Leed asked him, "Dad, do you need us to help you on the truck?" Telford said, "No, I just have to put this voltage regulator on where it'll charge the battery right." "Well, can we borrow the pickup for a while then?" asked Benji. "Sure," came his dad's answer.

Leed said "Let's go!" and they got into the truck. Benji asked, "Where we goin'?" Leed said, "To grandpa's to get some soap."

Benji looked puzzled and asked, "What fer?" Leed said, "I'm going to teach you what friction is, or ain't." Again Benji asked, "Why we going to Grandpas to get soap then?" Leed grinned and said, "Do you remember last fall when Grandma made them big bars of soap out of tallow and Red Devil Lye, and how bad it smelled, and how grandpa hid most of it out in the barn." Benji then smiled and said, "Oh, that soap."

They slipped into the barn and got two big bars of the lye soap and got back in the truck and took off. Benji, still not sure what was going on, asked, "Now where we going and what are we gonna do?" Leed answered, "Well we're going up to Tiger then down to Bethel Church and I'll show you how friction works, or don't work in this case." "Well how does it work? You've kept me in the dark long enough about this friction stuff."

Leed said, "Well friction is what makes stuff hard to slide, everything has a coefficient of friction about it, the smooth stuff has a low coefficient of friction while rough stuff has a real high coefficient of friction. But the weight of something also plays into how hard it is to slide. A coefficient of friction of one means you might as well just pick it up because you have to pull with the same power that it weighs to move it. So something that is light but has a low coefficient of friction will slide easy, but something that is heavy even though it has a low coefficient of friction, it will be hard to slide." He grinned at his brother, "You'll see. Now something that is heavy and has a high coefficient of friction like a log, well you might as well forget about slidin' it. You're just as well to get a couple of mules a hold of it, if you have to slide it."

Benji said, "Yeah I thank I got that but what's the soap fer?" Leed answered, "Well, smooth steel has a small coefficient of friction and a train track and the wheels of the train are made of steel. Right? Benji nodded his head. Leed continued, "But they have a whole lot of weight and that creates enough friction to pull a whole train out of Clayton and down along Stekoa Creek, even up the grade from Bethel, all the way into Tiger. Right?" Benji nodded again. Leed finished with, "Well, I'm going to show you what happens when we use the lye soap to really lower the coefficient of friction on the train tracks up that grade.

They went on into Tiger and took the short cut by driving up Blair Street and by the Presbyterian Church, the depot and Tiger

Elementary School and on down the road along the railroad tracks to Bethel Baptist Church. When they got almost to the church they turned left on the road that led back to the Ice Plant, and then parked in behind the old Jones House.

They got out, each with a bar of soap and ran around to where the Ice Plant Road crossed the railroad track. They walked up the track a good ways to where the grade picked up and Leed told Benji, "You put your bar of soap on that track and I'll put mine on this track and we'll push them and coat the track until we run out. The train is due in just a few minutes, so we better hurry!" The boys bent over and placed their bars on each track and took off. Benji got ahead so Leed poured it on and they raced all the way up for nearly fifty yards before the bars wore out in the middle. They crammed the two ends together and made it a little farther, before finally standing up to throw the remaining pieces away. Then they headed up into the woods to watch.

They rubbed their hands on leaves to get rid of the lye soap smell, then crouched behind trees a few yards apart, finally laying on the ground. Soon they heard the train coming and they stretched their necks around the tree to watch the show. The old Tallulah Falls Railroad trains never did move fast, but this one was a moving right along, until it hit the lye soap section of the track. As soon as the drive wheels were up on the soaped area, they started spinning like crazy and kept spinning as the momentum of the train kept it moving up the hill. The train made it almost to the end of the soaped section of the track before it stopped.

Leed and Benji had their necks still run out until the train stopped and the engineer bailed out. Then they slid around behind the tree completely, to disappear. The engineer and his helper were talking, "Yeah, it's soap. Them kids are at it again. Let's get the traction sand." They got out sacks of sand and poured it for several yards behind the drive wheels and for several yards in front of the drive wheels. Then they let the train roll back on the sanded section behind them to coat the wheels, before easing forward. They slowly built speed and then eased up the grade on into Tiger on their way back to Cornelia.

After they left Benji ran over and said, "I know what they used the sand fer."

"What?" asked Leed.

19

"It was to raise the coefficient of friction of the track and wheels enough so that they could drive off, because sand is rough."

"Great!" exclaimed Leed, "you're right!" They both smiled as they walked back down the track to the road and out to the truck. As they walked, Leed thought, "Well it worked, I taught him something!" Then he laughed inside.

CHAPTER

3

CATS

Saturday came and after working with their dad all morning, Leed and Benji cleaned up and went to town. The movie theater had a surfing film playing for the matinee, and since neither boy had ever seen a surfing movie, Benji was taken by how much fun it looked. Leed, on the other hand, looked at it with his characteristic engineering mind, and thought of a use for those skis Mr. Thurmond had given them.

On the way home Leed shared with Benji his idea he had about the skis, "We can make some small surf boards and take the binding off of the skis and put them on the surf boards and go surfing."

Benji queried, "Where are we going to find any waves around here?" "We're not," Leed answered, "we're going to surf down the side of the mountains on leaves and pine needles. That's what the bindings are for, to help us stay on the surf boards."

"Wow," Benji exclaimed, "that could be a lot of fun, scootin' down the side of a mountain, well, till you meet up with a big old oak tree while you'er slidin'. Now that could get your attention. And that really ain't surfin' no how, there ain't even no water."

"You'er right," said Leed, "we'll have to call them something else. Let's see, what did you say right then? Scootin'? That's a good name 'scoot boards'."

When they got home Leed went to the desk and got out some paper and started drawing the design for the scoot boards. After a couple of hours he went to Benji and said, "We got a problem. I got a design, but to make it work, we need some money to buy hardware and varnish to build and finish the scoot boards."

"How much?"

Leed said, "Four or five dollars I guess."

Benji with concern, "But we ain't got but two dollars between us and dad and mom don't never have no extra money neither." "Well I guess we'll just have to find a way to make some money," finished Leed.

The next Friday they knocked off of work early so Telford and Linda could go over to Hiawassee to see her sister. Just before they left, Linda told the boys, "Go over to your grandparents for supper, and don't stay up too late tonight."

When they arrived at Jeremiah and Ruby's house, Leed said, "We're here for supper cause mom and dad went over to Hiawassee to Aunt Janelle's to visit."

Ruby said, "That's good, I's about to start supper any how." Jeremiah asked, "I wonder why your mom's sister moved all the way over on the other side of the government trail fer? Well I guess it's all right, she married one of them Eller boys over there and they shore is hard workers, always goin' ninety miles an hour."

Jeremiah went in the kitchen to get a big fry pan down for Ruby and Benji asked Leed, "Why does grandpa call the Appalachian Trail the government trail fer?" Leed thought a second and answered, "Well I guess he was a middle age man during the Depression. That was when the government set up all of the CCC camps around here and built the Appalachian Trail, Rabun Beach and Campground and a lot of other trails, roads and stuff. So to him it was the government, building a government trail, on government land."

Benji nodded, "That makes sense."

Ruby was just starting to prepare supper on the wood cook stove. Leed and Benji sat down at the kitchen table with their grandpa and got to watch a real show unfold. As soon as Ruby started rattling pots and pans, the large number of cats that grandma had started pouring in the hole, over the couch, where the widow pane that Jeremiah had knocked out when he shot at Slewfoot, used to be. The cats immediately congregated at Ruby's feet and started rubbing around on the thick stockings that she wore over her legs all the time. This irritated her to no end, so she fetched the keen hickory that she still kept above the kitchen door, and had used on Leed and Benji a few times in years past.

She took the hickory and commenced to whuppin' on them cats, and as she waded through them they began to make themselves scarce. Some of the quicker thinking cats headed for the living room and dug their claws in the rug, turned and jumped onto the couch cushion, then onto the back of the couch and sailed out through the hole left by the missing window pane, where they had entered. As the other cats saw the escape route they followed as Ruby kept the pressure on them until the house was empty of cats. She immediately exclaimed, "I got to get rid of most of them cats and I'd pay good money to get it done!" Leed, sensing an immediate revenue source, spoke up, "How much would you pay to get rid of em?" She looked at him with her eyes still sparking and said, "I'll give you boys twenty five cents a head for every cat ye catch and haul to some other part of Rabun County." Leed said, "That's a deal!"

Ruby went back to cooking and since the house was getting hot, the boys went outside and ended up climbing up into the big white pine by the house and sitting on the limbs and cooling it. Benji looked from his limb to Leed on his limb and said, "How we gon'a catch them cats? Catchin' cats is hard." Leed answered, "I got an idea." When supper was ready Ruby stepped outside and hollered for the boys. They looked down and answered. She looked up at the boys in the tree and a fretful look come in her eyes and she said, "I told ye and I told ye about climbing in that tree. Now if you fall out of that thang and break yer leg, don't come runnin' to me! Now get down from there and come in this house and eat."

After supper, Leed and Benji went into the living room and sat down with their grandpa to talk. As was Jeremiah's custom, he kept the boys spellbound for the next hour telling about his experiences.

He started with, "Back when I was in my early thirties and in my prime, I got a job working with Georgee Power Company helping build Mathis Dam, which backs up Lake Rabun. I made good money, too, and that's how we bought this farm and this house. But anyway, when they had hired up a bunch of white folks down there, they still needed a lot more help, because they had so many people already workin' down in Tallulah Gorge on that big power plant down there. So they went down to Atlanter and hired up a bunch of black folks to keep the work a goin'. The white men give the black men a lots of trouble, and I don't know why, cause they's good workers and treated me real good. So to keep trouble down they built a camp for the black folks over there, and made that camp off limits to the whites.

"They's this one black guy that became a fast friend of mine, his name was Freeman Long from Atlanter, and he was real good at do'in most anythang and so was I. So we would get our heads together and figure thangs out so that they's this one Georgee Power engineer that would come and ask me and Freeman to take a walk with him when he was'a hav'in trouble with some'in and needed help, but did'nt want nobody to know about it. Me and Freeman would talk about it fer a while and tell that engineerin' guy how to do what he asked and he shore would thank us, but he always asked us to keep our business with him quiet. Guess he didn't want to look bad.

"After the dam was finished around 1915, I did pretty good logging on up into the twenties. Then they come back and built this here tunnel from Lake Rabun just above Mathis Dam through the mountain. These fellers started blasting on each side of the mountain in 1923, and about nine months later in 1924, they met underneath that mountain and them tunnels weren't off no more than a half inch from each other. Now that right there was some more piece of work. They built penstocks and the Terroa Power Plant at the low end of the tunnel, on the other side of the mountain from Mathis Dam. I got a job fer a while helping build the power house, buildin' forms for cement pours and stuff like that.

"Then the hard times hit and nobody made no money through the thirties, so I had to find a way to make money to feed Ruby and help your uncle, your dad, and the girls. I couldn't find nuttin' so I turned to bootleggin'. Well, so did every body else and the competition was stiff in the bootleggin' business around here. It was so bad that they used to call Tiger 'Fruit Jar City', because they unloaded so many fruit jars off the train there. In fact you boys know where Syrup City Road up there in Tiger is, don't ye? You know it runs from the city limit sign on US 441, over at a angle to the city limit sign on Bridge Creek Road." The boys said, "Shore." "Well they was four families that lived on Syrup City Road back then, and three of them was in the bootleggin' business. In fact one of them fellers had a well and he kept a jug of white liquor hung down in that well on a stout string where it stayed cool. If'n you didn't have enough money to buy a bottle of liquor, then he would pull that jug up out of the well and pour a lil' ol' dipper he had full and sell it to you fer 25¢.

"Now with that kind of competition I knowed that I had to come up with something that give me a leg up on the other fellers around here, that was a bootleggin'. Well, the guys out of town, like in Toccoa, or Royston and Gainesville, would pay a little more money if they knowed that they could depend on you to deliver good, clean liquor, from a copper still, that was the same from jar to jar, and didn't have no backin's in it."

Benji asked, "What's backin's?"

Jeremiah answered, "After you have soaked your ground corn and added the sugar and malt or yeast and let it work, and it's turned to mash, it's ready to run in the still. Then you load the still and bile the mash and catch the alkehol vapors coming off the mash. Now you run it through a copper tube that goes round and round in a barrel runnin' with cold water from a branch, so that it condenses and runs out as pure alkehol." He made a circling motion with his hand to show how the copper tube coiled in the barrel. "There comes a time when most of the alkehol is gone out of the mash and the other stuff in thar starts to bile off and mix with the last of the alkehol and they call that backin's. Now if you stop too soon then you lose alkehol and money but if you go too long, you bottle up backin's and lose customers, cause it looks and smells like liquor, but it feels thick in your mouth and it'll make you throw up." He puckered up and made a face to show how bad the backin's were.

"Well when I'm stuck with a problem I get'ta thank'in how can I fix this, so I thought water has a gravity about it."

Leed injected, "That's specific gravity grandpa."

"Yeah, that's right son," answered Jeremiah, "and alkehol has a gravity, 'pacific gravity' about it too and it's less than water, and backin's had to be somewhere in between the two, I thought. So if I could build a balancing device, and fill one end with water, and run the liquor through the other end, and make it real delecate, then the heavier water would keep it tilted one way and the liquor that was a comin' out after condensing would go down to be bottled. But when the backin's started runnin through the balance device, it would tilt toward the other end where the heavier backin's was and would dump the backin' down to the ground and I would stop the process right there."

"Did it work?" Benji asked.

"Shore did," answered Jeremiah, "after moving the see-saw point back and forth till I got it just right."

"What did you call it grandpa?" asked Benji.

"The 'Hydro-Balance-Separator'," smiled grandpa, "cause it used water which, I learnt from Georgee Power is called hydro, and balance, and it separated the alkehol and the backin's."

"Where is it now?" asked Leed.

Jeremiah thought for a minute and said, "Well, that thang made me a lot of money. Everybody trusted my liquor because of it, but up during the war the Army was a buy'in all the lumber they could get, and payin' a good price fer it, too. So I retired the still and the hydro balance separator and put them up in the top of the barn and bought a newer truck and started logging fer a livin'. Then later I took notice that your uncle Latimer seemed to have a lot of money and I checked in the barn, and the still and the 'hydro-balance-separator' was gone. I can't find em, cause Latimer has 'em hid som'wheres. I'd feel better if he would'nt do'in nuttin' like that, but he turned out real hard headed and had'nt listen to me in years."

When Jeremiah was through he went into the kitchen to get another cup of coffee and Leed stood up, rubbed his behind and said, "I shore do like grandpa's stories, but settin' fer that long in these straight back chairs, with them oak strips woven together for a seat, shore is hard on your bottom."

It was getting dark so Leed and Benji told Jeremiah and Ruby goodnight and started walking home. On the way Benji asked

27

Leed, "Why does Grandpa smell the way he does? Dad and me and you don't smell like that?"

Leed answered, "Well I thank it's just bein' an old man and not takin' a bath much. Most old men smell like that. In fact, we can check this out tomorrow when we go to the feed store with dad."

4 FEED STORE

The next morning, after breakfast, the boys and their dad loaded up in the truck and headed to town to pick up feed and fertilizer. When they got to the feed store, the owner of the store, old Mr. Frank, as everyone called him, was sitting behind the counter on the left. Leed and Benji looked with amazement at Mr. Frank, who had his false teeth out and was picking food particles out from between each teeth with a sharp pencil. They tried not to stare, but it was quite a sight. As they followed their dad, he looked at each old man sitting around on the barrels and piles of feed sacks and said hello, then addressed each of them. As he moved along, he said, "Hello J. C." "R. E." "L. M." "J. L." "C. J." "Bill" "Hub, how are ya'll doing." Benji followed Leed off to the side and quietly asked him, "Why don't none of them old men have a real name?" Leed answered the best he could with, "I don't know, maybe they done so much bad stuff back when they was young that they're tryin' to hide their name or somethin'."

As Telford and the old men took turns talking, the boys decided to get down to the business at hand of finding out if all old men smelled like grandpa. They would work their way along behind each old man as easy as they could and sniff a bit, then look at each other and nod in agreement that they all smelled like grandpa. They ended up back near the front door, opposite of Mr. Frank, who now had his teeth in and was feeling a mite frisky.

About that time the door opened and in walked another old man who stopped and looked straight at Mr. Frank, and said, "I got something on you Mr. Frank. I bet I can tell ye what'cha had fer breakfast this morning." Mr. Frank not to be outdone answered, "Bet'cha can't." Now everyone in the store was lisenting, as the man said, "Bet'cha I can. You had eggs this morning because they're still on your chin." Everyone laughed because Mr. Frank was hard to get. But Mr. Frank come right back and answered, "You're wrong, had eggs yesterday morning." The whole place just roared and the old man who had just come in the door admitted defeat by hanging his head and goin' to set down. Just as he sat down the feller named R. E. said, "Don't feel whupped down, Lester, we all know you're a level-headed feller, cause that snuff juice runs out of both sides of your mouth at the same time." Another round of laughter followed, as Lester just shook his head.

Leed had noticed one of the old men smoking as they came in, and he was amazed at how fast he rolled a new smoke. When he wanted another smoke he, without even paying half attention, reached into his overall bib with his right hand, pulled out a pack of wrapping papers and slid out a single paper with his left hand. He then put up the pack of papers and pulled out his flat can of Prince Albert tobacco, all with what looked like one motion. He creased the paper around his left pointing finger, while holding the end with his next finger and thumb. With one fluid motion he flipped open the lid on the Prince Albert can with his thumb and sprinkled the tobacco onto the paper and closed the lid as he slid it back into the bib of his overalls. At the same time, he had already rolled the paper and tobacco into a cigarette with his left hand and was licking the paper down so it would hold together. In the same motion he used to lick the paper, he turned the cigarette and hung it on his lip. With his right hand he had already pulled out a small match box and he immediately lit the PA cigarette and was smoking. From the time he pulled out the pack of papers until he was smoking was no more than six or eight seconds. Leed was fascinated with the mechanics and timing that the old man had developed to sustain his smelly habit.

Leed and Benji looked out the door and saw that their uncle Latimer and his twin boys, who were Leed"s age, were coming toward the door. Latimer was a mean looking, rough skinned fellow who was a pretty keen businessman, but was also crooked and over-bearing. His twin sons were Ronnie, who was fat and dumb like his mother, Gleyniss' side of the family, but he wanted to be tough and overbearing like his father. Since no one took him serious, he was domineering to his brother, Lonnie, who was in front of him. Lonnie was fat also, and dumber than dirt, but he was a lot more likable than his brother. His only real friend was his dog and constant companion, a hound named Jeff, that he had left in the back of his dad's pickup. As Lonnie threw the door open and came in, Mr. Frank said something and Lonnie, the only one who heard him, looked funny at Mr. Frank, then came on over to where everyone was talking.

After Latimer was in the store and everyone was listening, Telford, being a proud father, told the story about how the log truck had gotten stuck. He explained that Leed had figured out how to hook the chain from the wheel to the crossbeam and how they got out of the mud hole. Everyone smiled with approval, except Latimer and Ronnie, and he even elbowed Lonnie for smiling. Latimer quickly did his business and left with the twins boys, because he wasn't the sociable type.

After they left, the guy named J. C. told about Latimer and how he stole the still and 'hydro-balance-separator' from Jeremiah and used it to get rich and how many people and families were hurt by drinking liquor. He allowed as to how Latimer and his boys were running the still somewhere back in the mountains, behind the farm that Jeremiah had given him.

The old feller named Hub spoke up and said, "Well now, I shore am glad I quit drankin' liquor. When I coundn't get no government liquor to drank, then I was a getting' white liquor. Before I quit, I was stuck on that stuff bad, even though I could handle it pretty good." R. E. smacked his leg and said, "Well Hub, ye know better'n that, why I remember a long time ago, if'n ye set down on a rotten apple ye wouldn't be able to talk plain for an hour." Everybody laughed as Hub huffed at R. E.

Leed had listened intently to what J. C. had said, because he didn't like for bad things to go on, especially that close to where he lived. It really bothered him. He also wondered why someone didn't do something about Latimer and his still. After the talk settled down, Telford and the boys concluded their business, loaded the truck and headed back home.

The boys spent the evenings during the next week, except Wednesday when they all went to church, in their father's shed working down three pieces of dry black-gum which they had split out of a big block of wood. Because of its criss-cross grain, black-gum was the toughest wood available to make the scoot boards out of. Also because of its density, they were able to work it down to an extremely smooth finish. By the end of the week they had the three pieces worked down, sanded and ready for the varnish and the hardware to fasten the ski binders to the boards.

Friday, after work, the boys told their mom that they were going to go to their grandmother's for supper. Actually, the real reason was to catch cats to make money. When they arrived at their grandparent's house they told their grandma she had better get the egg money bowl out, cause they were there to catch cats. She said, "Well you better be ready to run 'cause them cats is hard to catch."

Leed answered, "We ain't going to use our feet grandma, we're going to use our heads to catch them cats." They went straight out to the shed and got a big tow sack, an old large, straight sided pot with the bottom rusted out, a pair of pliers and a tack hammer.

Benji asked, "What's all this fer?"

Leed answered, "Just do what you're told and we'll have the money tonight."

They walked back in the house and sat away from the couch and waited on grandma to start supper. As the pans started rattling, the cats poured in through the hole where the window pane was gone. Leed counted seventeen cats and knew that they were all in. He told Benji, "Let's go." They quickly went outside and used the pliers to pull the tacks out of a window pane, which they quickly used to replace the middle pane that was missing where the cats had come in. They used the hammer to drive the tacks in to hold the pane securely. They quickly went back into the house, eased in behind the couch and sat down out of sight. Leed positioned Benji and himself below and on each side of the window pane that had been missing, but was now replaced, then positioned the tow sack between him and Benji. They eased the large straight sided pot down into the sack and held the top of the sack at the top of the pot, and then raised it up right behind the top of the back of the couch and waited.

Jeremiah had been standing back in the bedroom watching with great interest and now that he had figured out what was going on, he was watching with much anticipation and a big smile, as he thought about how smart this grandson of his was.

As Leed and Benji waited, they heard a great commotion in the kitchen as grandma moved into action and started whuppin' on them cats with her hickory. Jeremiah watched with glee as the first cats rushed into the living room, dug their claws into the carpet and leaped for the couch cushion then the back of the couch and sailed toward what they thought was an opening. But the cats, one after another, hit the glass with a thud and fell straight down the throat of the big pot into the sack. The pot being metal didn't allow the cats to climb out easily. To keep them from even trying, Leed and Benji each used his free hand to shove the captured cats into the bottom of the large sack back under the couch.

Finally, one cat saw the open window and made a leap for it, followed quickly by the two remaining cats.

Jeremiah hollered, "You got'em, close the sack, only three of em got out the winder!" Leed and Benji immediately slid the pot up and closed the sack quickly. The captors came out from behind the couch with a big sack of cats to be welcomed by a wide grin and a, "You done good boys, I'm proud of ye both!" from their grandpa.

Ruby came out of the kitchen about that time and asked, "How many did ye get?"

Leed answered, "Fourteen."

"How much do I owe ya then?" was Ruby's quick reply.

Leed who was quick on math came right back with, "Three dollars and fifty cents."

Ruby said, "OK, but you still got to haul em off."

"That'll be fine," said Leed. "Grandpa, can we borrow yer truck after supper to haul the cats off?"

"Sure," Jeremiah answered, "where are ye taking em?"

"We thought we'd go up to Tiger and then on up Bridge Creek

Road and starting there at the Suzie Shirley place, drop off a male and a female at each farm up the road as long as they last."

"That sounds good son," answered Jeremiah.

After supper Ruby paid the boys $3.50, then Leed and Benji hauled the cats off. As they got rid of the cats, they talked a lot during the drive. Leed shared with Benji his concern that no one was doing anything about their uncle Latimer breaking the law and teaching their cousins to do the same.

Benji's answer drove deep into Leed's sensitive heart, "Why does someone else have to do something? Don't you think we might be able to do something too?"

Leed pondered this in his mind on the way back to their grandparents and then as they walked home, and even as he lay in bed that night, concerning what to do about the law breaking that his uncle and cousins were doing. But just before he dozed off he decided to be more cautious than his daring brother, and talk it over with his dad the next day.

The next morning at breakfast Benji told his dad and mom about Leed's idea and catching the cats and earning the $3.50. Leed asked if they could borrow the truck to go to town to get supplies to finish the scoot boards that afternoon. Then Leed got a real serious look on his face and asked, "Dad, if Uncle Latimer and Ronnie and Lonnie have a still near here, then why don't we cut it down and destroy grandpa's 'hydro-balance-separator'?"

Telford got a real serious look on his face and then said, "Well son, there's two reasons. One, your uncle is mean and someone could get hurt if it started a war between our families, so we don't need to go there. And two, even if I knew no one would get hurt, I don't want to strain what little relationship I have with my older brother. I love him and he's been a having some real problems the last few months and I think he has cancer. Worse than that, if he dies in the state he's in, then he's not ready. I've talked with him about Jesus and how God's word clearly states that Jesus is the only way, and he won't listen but just gets belligerent. So right now, I'm going to just pray for Latimer."

Leed's eyes shot back and forth as he tilted his head down and thought about his dad's statement, because he himself wondered how there could only be one way to heaven and why Jesus was that way.

The kitchen was tense so Leed got up and told Benji, "Let's go," and they left for town. As they neared town on the way to Reeves Hardware to get the parts, Benji exclaimed, "There's Loge Rogers, wave at him, he's on your side!" But Leed was in deep thought and did not even acknowledge that Benji had spoke. Benji just settled back and kept quiet.

After they left Reeves, Leed finally spoke, "Benji, you was right, if dad or nobody else will do nothing about Latimer, then I guess it is up to you and me. Will you go with me tonight to hunt for the still?"

"Sure. I think I know where it is. About two years ago I saw where somebody buried a pipe from the branch up on the government land, around the mountain into that stand of pines behind Latimer's barn, just above the government line. I figure that has to be where the still is because they hid that pipe pretty good when they buried it and you can't even tell where it is now."

Leed said, "Good we'll handle this problem tonight."

Leed and Benji varnished the scoot boards three times that afternoon and after supper, they got everything ready to assemble after a good drying period. Their mom stepped out of the back of the house awhile before dark and said, "We're going to Bill and Gertrude's, would y'all like to come?" They both said, "No."

After their mom had gone back into the house, Benji said, "Whew, I sure didn't want to go down there and watch mom and Gertrude put bobby pins in each others hair so they'll look good in church tomorrow."

"Me neither," replied Leed, "besides that, now we can go find that still without making up a story."

Leed and Benji left the shed, before dark, carrying an axe so they could chop up the still when they found it. At about the same time on the farm nearby, Latimer looked at Ronnie and said, "Son, I don't feel good this evening, but it's Saturday night and someone might get out and mess around up at the still. Would you take that 22 pump and go up and watch things till about eleven o'clock?"

"Yeah dad," answered Ronnie feeling real big and holding his chest out as he grabbed the gun from the gun rack and started loading it. Latimer, never one to let anybody feel like somebody, looked back at Ronnie and said, "And don't shoot yourself, you idiot, shoot whoever comes around."

Ronnie frowned as he went out the door and slammed it behind him. As he walked up the ridge behind the barn he talked to himself, "I'll show him, I'm tough as he is!"

Leed and Benji sat back against two trees waiting for the moon to light the woods, then they started slipping into where they now knew the still was. One of them stepped on a stick, just a few yards from the still, causing it to make a loud 'crack'. Ronnie, who was sitting on a stool in the still house dozing, jumped up, startled, scared half to death and shouted, "Who is it?" He threw the gun up and started shooting in the direction of the noise. The first bullet hit a small pine tree about eight inches from Leed's face and threw bark in his right eye. He grabbed his eye, turned, crouched low and started running. Bullets were hitting in the trees all around him. He finally heard Benji out ahead of him, moving real fast, so he fell in behind him and they didn't stop running until they were back on their own farm and safe. As they stopped Benji dropped the axe, which he had carried the whole time, started laughing and said, "Whew that was close." As he turned, the moon light shining on Leed's face revealed a right eye that was tearing from the bark and a left eye full of fear.

Leed was trembling, and said in a far away voice, "We... we could have been killed."

"And you ain't even ready to go, are you?" came Benji's somber reply. They walked down to the spring in silence, where Leed washed out his eye. Then they went on home and Leed went straight to bed, where he tried to talk to God but he didn't know what to say. He wondered how his dad could talk so freely to God yet he couldn't even formulate words when he tried to pray. He lay stiff 'till morning and got only a little fitful sleep.

Leed was very quiet at breakfast and as they all got ready and went to church. Preacher Bill, an endearing term for their pastor, preached out of Romans, Chapter 5, but it didn't make sense to Leed, as his mind whirled, from the incident the night before, to what Preacher Bill was saying, to the things that Leed thought about life in general.

After he got through preaching, Preacher Bill, as he always did, gave an invitation and Leed wanted to go forward and talk to him, but he just couldn't get himself to move from where he was standing. His brother, mom and dad all were looking at his white knuckles as he held onto the pew in front of them. As they all prayed for him, his dad kept whispering, "Help him Father, help him."

As they headed home, Leed's mind kept going back to that one verse that Preacher Bill had started with that day. Romans 5:1 stuck in Leed's mind and he kept wondering how he could have that peace with God that the verse talked about. Was this peace with God to be obtained through Jesus Christ alone as this verse said?

5

FOURTH OF JULY

The next day, after the boys were through helping their dad log, they went out to the barn to do the chores. As they rounded the corner of the barn with Benji in the lead, they scattered a flock of new biddies. The mama game hen immediately came to their aid by flapping up in the air and coming at Benji's face with her spurs out and meaning business. Benji immediately covered his face and dropped to the ground hollering.

Leed ran the hen off and grabbed Benji by the arm and said, "Stand up, she's gone." After Benji got up, Leed looked at him and said, "You ain't afraid to die but you are afraid of a settin' hen. Why?" Benji, with a sheepish look on his face answered, "I have Jesus in my heart and I know Him as a friend and the Bible tells me that knowing Jesus is eternal life, so I ain't afraid to die. But now settin' hens always go fer yer eyes, and I don't want to hang around down here blind." Leed looked kind of half way puzzled and said "I'll have to think about that."

They went on about their chores. Benji fed the livestock while Leed threw some scratch feed out to the chickens, and then took a basket while the chickens were eating and went to gather the eggs. They had a lot of game chickens so there were a lot of nests with eggs. Telford had told them to leave the nests in the hen house alone to allow those hens to raise more chickens, so there would be plenty of fried chicken later in the summer and fall. But these game chickens were innovative and had nests all over the place. Leed liked the challenge of finding a nest back in the hay, under some equipment, in the top of the barn, even behind the pile of lumber they had in one stall. With the henhouse off limits, he still got several eggs in the basket that he took to his mom who washed them and put them in a tray she had especially for eggs.

The next morning Latimer told Ronnie and Lonnie, "Boys, we got to look like we have some income to keep the federal boys off of us, so we got to load some logs today to sell to keep up a good pretense."

Lonnie asked, "What's a pretense?"

Latimer looked mean at him and said, "You don't need to know, let's go."

After a hard day of work, the twins had a good load of logs because they were pushed all day by their overbearing father, who was too sick to work much. Now they were coming down the road that separated their property from Telford's land. When Latimer came to the big mud-hole where Telford had gotten stuck, he didn't even slow down as he entered, but he got stuck in the same spot as Telford did anyway.

After getting out and surveying the situation, Ronnie said, "I know how to get it out, dad; Leed ain't the only smart one in this territory!"

Latimer, surprised said, "Good son, get it out then."

Ronnie did just what he had heard his uncle say that Leed had done, and soon he put Lonnie in the cab to drive the truck out of the mud hole. There was one slight detail, however that Ronnie wasn't aware of, and that was to feather the clutch to take up the slack in the chain slow. Spinning the wheels to take up the slack would create a lot of inertia, that would jerk the load down and sideways, so hard it would turn the truck over.

Ronnie and his dad walked up by the cab of the truck on the driver's side, which was also the side where the chain was hooked. Ronnie said to Lonnie, "Pour the painter pee to it, Lonnie." Lonnie obediently stomped the gas pedal and dumped the clutch at the same time. When all of the slack was taken out of the chain by the roaring engine and the spinning dual rear wheels, the truck jerked so violently it lurched up on its left side with a groan and started falling right toward Ronnie and Latimer. Ronnie staggered backward, fell, and knocked his dad to safety as the cab of the truck landed right by his feet. As the chain broke with a loud "pow", the logs rolled out on the ground next to Ronnie and Latimer making huge thuds as they rolled out of control for several seconds before it finally got quiet.

After the commotion was over, a scared-to-death Lonnie climbed out of the top of the truck like a big fat squirrel, and stood by his brother Ronnie, looking down at Latimer. When Latimer finally got up from where he had been laying, he said, "You boys have come un-slapped and I'm gonn'a fix that right now." He then snaked out his hand and commenced to slapping both of his twins with rough, hard blows that could be heard a long ways. Both boys took off for the house a-hollering, "It ain't our fault, Uncle Telford and Leed set us up and you know it!"

They hid in the barn loft 'til the next day, when they slipped down and into the kitchen for something to eat. They took the tractor after they ate and went back and spent a long day getting the truck and the logs out.

After church on Wednesday night, Leed and Benji, feeling young and energetic, asked if they could walk home since it was still over an hour before dark. Their parents agreed, so they headed down the road. When they came to the Potts farm, they decided to take the old road across the farm to cut about a quarter of a mile off their trip.

As they were passing below the Potts house at the low end of the pasture, they heard a pitiful wailing coming from behind some bushes near the pond. The boys slipped up with the hair on the back of their necks standing straight up. What they saw was Lisa Potts, the young wife of the second Potts boy, Larry, sitting by the pond crying loudly. As they looked on, she started talking to someone the boys couldn't see. "Yes honey, I see you." Then she got up. "Yes, I'm coming." The young woman started walking straight toward the deep part of the pond. Then she just stepped right out onto a water lily pad and dropped off into the pond, out of sight.

The boys were so shocked they didn't move until they saw her hand and the top of her head bob up and then back down. Benji, being the quickest one of the pair, ran at full speed toward the pond, slowed to flip off his shoes, then dove into the deep water. He quickly found Lisa and started moving her towards shore, even though she kept trying to go back into the deep. Leed, standing waist deep in the water on the side of the bank, was finally able to reach out and catch her hand and drag her to the bank. Leed held her by one arm until Benji got out and caught her by the other arm, to help him pull her out.

It took both of them to hold her as she kept trying to go back to the pond. "Let me go," she screamed, "I've got to go to her." Finally, they got her calmed down and walked her up to the house, where her mother-in-law got towels for her and the boys. After they finally got her settled in bed, Mrs. Potts said, "She had a baby still-born day before yesterday and she's a taken it real hard. Thank you boys for bein' there."

Benji answered, "You're welcome, we had her on the prayer list at church tonight."

Mrs. Potts thanked them again and they headed on home.

When they arrived home, late and wet, their dad asked, "What happened?" Benji explained the situation to his parents, then Leed, who had really been thinking about what had transpired that evening, asked, "Dad, who was she talking to, and why did she walk out on that water lily pad? She could have drowned!"

"You're right son," he answered, "she could have drowned. Well the way I see it is, the Potts are good folks but they don't never have no time for God. They just work on Sunday and don't go to church. So when something bad happens in this world, they don't have nobody to turn to, that can really help em, like Jesus can." He continued with concern in his eyes, "Like Lisa tonight. She has longed for that baby girl for the last two days and she finally started hearing and seeing things. If the Lord hadn't sent you two boys along, she would be dead now."

Leed asked, "Do you really think the Lord sent us by there tonight, dad?"

"Of course son, He is in control of everything. Just think... why did you and Benji want to walk home tonight? Why did you cut across the Potts farm and why did you arrive at just the right time to see Lisa go into the pond?"

As they continued to talk about it, Leed thought he would really like to have someone private to turn to himself. That thought stayed with him until he went to sleep.

The next morning Telford told the boys that since it was close to the Fourth of July, they wouldn't have to work again until the next week. Leed, in an anxious tone, said to Benji, "Let's get Tommy Hawk so we can try out the scoot boards!" Tommy Hawk was a Cherokee boy that lived down the road and across the creek. He was younger than Leed and Benji, but was still their best friend.

After they had gotten Tommy Hawk, each boy grabbed a scoot board and headed for Crumley Mountain. They stopped at the bottom of the big cove before it got too steep, so they could practice and learn how to use the scoot boards before attacking the mountain itself. After a lot of falls, they began getting the hang of Leed's new invention. First Benji, the most athletic, and Tommy Hawk, who was also very agile, started putting together some pretty long scoots with some good turns. Finally, Leed was able to stay up and dodge the trees for a couple of long runs. The boys practiced there at the bottom of the cove until they were tired, then went home to recoup and get ready for the Fourth of July celebration they were having at their house on Saturday.

Friday morning Linda told Leed and Benji to go out and pick two buckets of blackberries so she could make pies for the get-to-gether. Both boys were good at berry picking, but they didn't like the tedious task because of the briers that they grew on stuck you a lot and you had to fight your way through a lot of varmints to get the choice berries. You also had to watch out for wasp or hornet nests built in the denser stands of briers. Gnats would fly into your eyes, mosquitoes and no see-ums would bite you. Copperheads and even an occasional Rattler could also be found hiding in the briers.

Upon arriving home, Leed and Benji had to do a tick check, like they were two hound dogs. But worst of all were the chiggers that showed up as itchy red spots the next day. Chiggers were tiny bugs that got on you, then embedded themselves in the skin of your more sensitive body areas. They usually took a day to embed and start itching and they would stay with you for several days, if you didn't suffocate them. The quickest method they had found to get rid of them was to take their mom's fingernail polish and paint over the itchy area to cut off their oxygen and the almost invisible bugs would be gone the next day.

They courageously ventured into the blackberry thickets and, by mid-afternoon, brought back two good buckets full of berries. They suffered for the berries because they knew that the extra they had picked would be converted into that wonderful substance, blackberry jelly which, when combined with butter biscuits, was such an important part of a mountain breakfast in the fall and winter. Linda baked four pies from the berries that they had picked and made an entire batch of jelly.

That Saturday was the Fourth of July and everybody was coming over for a big get-together. Linda spent all day cooking a big meal for everybody. By the time everyone started arriving that afternoon, she had baked a big cured ham and two big hens. To go with all the meat she also cooked a big boiler full of pinto beans, a boiler of red taters, another of green beans, and the big fry pan full of gravy. To go on the side, she baked two cakes of corn bread and a huge platter of biscuits. Scattered around on the tables on the porch and outside were moulds of fresh butter, jars of jelly and jars of chow-chow and some of Jeremiah's hot cayenne peppers. After Telford blessed the food, all of the folks ate until they were beyond full and then everyone rested a while.

Leed lay back against a porch post too stuffed to move. There was nowhere else to sit, all the seats on the porch and outside were already taken by guests. He heard the old men talking about the war which interested him, since his two older brothers were over there. He listened close. One man said, "You know them Communists tried to cross the 38th parallel last month and we kicked 'em good and sent 'em back north. But I heered they was tryin' to do it again." Another man said, "I wish they'ed get that thang over with over there." "Yep, they might as well draw a line right there at that 38th parallel and cut that country in half, they ain't never gonna' get along no how," added another fellow. Then somebody else said, "Yeah, I think old Ike would like to end Truman's war and get our boys home, since they've about come to a draw over there."

Leed thought that would be good to get his brothers back state-side.

When it started cooling down, Leed's favorite part of the get-together was about to start. Some of Telford's folks and friend's got out their guitars, banjos, mandolins, and fiddles and commenced to tuning them up; Sam had even brought his big bass fiddle too. They soon gathered out on the porch where it was cool and start-ed playing bluegrass music to an audience that was sitting on the porch rails, in chairs on the porch, and out in the yard. Even a few of the kids were up in the maple tree listening.

Leed noticed one old fellow that had been picking the banjo for a long time played claw hammer style, with no picks, by just grabbing the strings like it had always been done. But one younger fellow had been off somewhere and learned that new three finger picking style, to pick with two finger picks and a thumb pick. Now they had been trying to out do one another for quite a while, when the other players finally just backed off and let them have it. The older fellow would pick a quick little ditty and then the younger fellow would play it right back to him, like he had always known it. As this went on, the ditties that the old fellow played got more involved and faster, but the younger fellow's answer was always right on. Now the crowd and the other players were getting into it, hollering and whooping, until finally the old feller and the young feller just grinned at each other and started playing together, soon to be joined by the other players.

The music went on until nearly midnight when the crowd start-ed to thin out and finally everybody went home. Leed went to bed tired, but thinking how much fun bluegrass music is, even if you can't play a lick.

6 FUNERAL

The next day at church, Telford heard that his brother, Latimer, had taken a turn for the worse. Upon returning home, he and Linda went into their bedroom and prayed for quite a while. After talking with the Lord, Telford left to go and talk to Latimer.

When he arrived, Gleyniss, his sister-in-law, showed him to the bedroom, just to the right of the front room, where Latimer was laying. Then she left. They exchanged pleasantries for a few moments and then the room got stony quiet. Telford shot a quick prayer up for courage and looked at Latimer and said, "Latimer, you are my brother and I love you and we both know that you don't have long to live. I've asked you before and I'm going to ask you again, 'do you know where you are going when you die?'"

Latimer snorted, "I don't care where I'm going!"

Telford looked sorrowfully at his brother and said, "You don't mean that Latimer. You have to stand before God after you die and you aren't ready for that." Latimer's answer was cold, "And why not? I'll work something out with Him when I get there." Telford, almost tearful now, and with pleading in his voice, said, "You won't even be allowed to speak when sinners are judged at the Great White Throne Judgment, and that's where you'll be if you don't have Jesus as your savior before you die."

Latimer swept with his hand and said, "Get out of here, I don't want to hear any more of this!" Again Telford pleaded, "Please Latimer don't go without Jesus, please?" Telford's eyes now full, ran over and the tears ran down his face as he got the last clouded look at his brother, as the dying man turned away his face, still sweeping with his hand for Telford to go. Telford wept all the way home and went into his bedroom and continued to weep for his brother that he knew he had lost.

Latimer did not talk to Gleyniss, Ronnie or Lonnie for most of the week, but just stared at the wall. Finally on Thursday evening, he started hollering for all of them to come there. He then told them to listen good, "Gleyniss, get all my money together and put it in the big jar with the crook handle on it. Boys,, after your mom puts the money in the jar I want you to take it upstairs and put it right above me." "But why daddy?" asked Ronnie. "So I can grab it on the way up and use it to bribe God when I get there," Latimer retorted.

"But what about us, and mom, we need money too?" asked Ronnie in a hurt tone. Latimer, now cold and demanding said, "I don't care! It's my money, now move, all of you!" Gleyniss and the twins obeyed Latimer's instructions with heavy hearts, painfully unable to resist him.

Nobody went back into Latimer's room until Gleyniss took his breakfast the next morning. As she entered the room, she saw he was slumped over in an unnatural way and she realized that he had died during the night. The sorrow and the pressure of being married to this horrible man for so many years mixed with the hard-to-grasp feeling of relief that the pressure might be over. It was all too much for Gleyniss, as her head started to spin. She dropped the plate of food and the cup of coffee she was carrying and just collapsed to the floor. Ronnie and Lonnie who were in the kitchen came running. As they rushed to their mom's side they looked and realized also that their dad was gone. After reviving their mom and helping her to the couch, Ronnie called the funeral home. Lonnie cleaned up the dropped breakfast even though he didn't like being in the room with a dead person. He kept thinking that his dad might turn into a ghost and start slapping him.

After the funeral director picked up the body, he asked Gleyniss if she could come by the funeral home at noon and make arrangements and pick out a casket. She said they would be there.

At noon, Ronnie and Lonnie took their mom to town and they all went to talk to the funeral director. After they sat down in his office, he started asking Gleyniss for details for the obituary. She was in such an emotional state that she broke down again. The funeral director quickly got his wife and had her take Gleyniss to the lounge to recover.

He then returned to the boys and looked at them, as he asked, "You both appear to be mature young men. Can you help me get some details about your father?" They both nodded yes. He asked them for all of the sundry information and Ronnie answered. Then he asked, "Do you know anything unusual or special about your father?" Ronnie said, "No."

But Lonnie, realizing this was a question he could answer, spoke up and said, "He had two butt holes!" Ronnie looked at Lonnie totally stunned and the startled funeral director fell back in his chair as his glasses slid down his nose. He looked over his lens and asked, "And how did you come about this bit of information, might I ask?" Lonnie answered, "Well every time me and Ronnie went to the feed store with dad, I'd go in first and old Mr. Frank would always say, 'There comes that Latimer Brown with them two butt holes.'"

The funeral director almost choked trying to keep from laughing, while Ronnie's look turned mean and he snorted, "You idiot, he was talking about you and me, not dad." Lonnie, with a puzzled look replied, "But we ain't got two butt holes Ronnie; we're twins and I've seen you naked." Ronnie slapped Lonnie and raised his voice and said, "Shut up, you idiot."

Lonnie whined, "Don't hit me, everybody hits me. I don't like being hit." About that time Gleyniss came back and Ronnie pushed Lonnie to the front of the funeral home to shut him up while their mom finished with the formalities.

The funeral was Sunday afternoon. Only Gleyniss, the twins, Jeremiah, Ruby, Telford, his family, his two sisters and some of their family came to Latimer's funeral, which was preached by the funeral director. It was short, and sweet, with very little substance. After they put him in the ground, Gleyniss and the boys came back to the big empty house drained of all energy and emotion.

They just sat in the front room for a long time, not even talking. Finally, Ronnie hollered, "The jar!" The three of them ran upstairs to where the jar had been. After charging into the room they stopped and looked at the jar sitting right where the boys had placed it, still full of money. Finally, Lonnie broke the silence with, "Maybe we should have put it in the cellar." Ronnie reached out and slapped his brother and said, "Shut up, you idiot!"

Lonnie whined, "Don't hit me." His mother said, "Oh shut up!" as she grabbed the handle of the jar full of money and headed to her bedroom.

The next day two men came in a big car and talked to Gleyniss out on the porch. After awhile, she went into the kitchen and talked to Ronnie and Lonnie, "Boys, those two men out there have made a pretty good offer on the still and that separator thang. Do you think we should sell it?"

Ronnie immediately answered, "No! We know how to run that still, and we're just as good a business-men as dad. If you sell it, we won't have no income, well not no good income anyhow. We better keep it, mom; we have to keep you up now." She looked at Ronnie, nodded then went back out on the porch and sent the men away.

On Tuesday Telford told the boys, "We have to hoe the corn again and side-dress it so we'll have a crop this fall. That's our food and the food for the livestock along with the hay and fodder. We better take off a couple of days and get it done."

Both boys looked less than excited. Logging was hard work, but it was a challenge, so it kept you interested. Hoeing corn was a real drag. They got their hoes and went out into the field where they started at the top of the field and each took a row. It was hot work and the only thing that Leed and Benji had to look forward to was the end of the row they were on. Still another row was always waiting. After lunch the next day they had the rows hoed out and their dad had been plowing out the middles with Ben the mule.

After he finished, he told Benji to take Ben, un-harness him and turn him out into the pasture, while he and Leed started side dressing the corn with ammonia nitrate. In a few minutes Leed looked and Benji was out in the pasture scoot boarding behind the mule as he ran through the pasture. Benji had dropped the plow and gotten his scoot board out and was now in the pasture holding on to the single tree and the reins at the same time. Ben was taking him for a pretty good ride. In a minute Telford looked and saw what Benji was doing and hollered and told him to un-harness the mule, rub him down and get back to work.

Friday evening Jeremiah came down to the house and told everybody, "I heered the first katydids the other night, so that means its three months to frost. Let's see, I heered em on Monday night, that was the thirteenth, so its gonna frost on the thirteenth of October. Now that's just a mite late fer the first frost, and the wooly worms ain't got no wide strips this year, so that means we're gonna have a mild winter."

Telford said, "That's good, dad, but we still need to cut and split some more wood fer the winter." "Yeah, you're right son, we better stay at it fore it gets cold," answered Jeremiah.

Come Saturday, Leed and Benji made a trip back to Lake Rabun with their cut off jeans between them on the seat. After seeing Benji scoot boarding behind the mule, Leed had an idea. They were going to try to find someone to pull them and let them use the scoot boards on the water.

They stopped by Lake Rabun Boat Dock and stood around awhile, asking people who were putting in if they were going skiing but they were all in a hurry to get to their lake houses. After a good long while, they were talking about leaving when they heard a powerful boat come around the point and then back off to ease into the dock area. It was Danielle. Leed's heart leaped as she pulled up and told the dock attendant to fill up her dad's boat.

Leed and Benji came over and showed her the scoot boards that

Leed had invented, using the ski binding from the skis that her dad had given them. Leed wanted to ask her to ski but Benji beat him to it. He asked her, "We want to try them out today on the water, are you going skiing this afternoon?" She smiled and said, "Yes, dad was going to drive for me later, but we can go show him Leed's invention and tell him that you can drive for me. He won't mind; he always has some business stuff in his briefcase to work on."

The boys went into the store and put on their cut off jeans and put their clothes in the truck. They hopped in the boat and Danielle drove around to the Stone Place. She ran up and got her dad; he came down and really thought that Leed's invention was neat. He had no problem with Leed and Benji going skiing with Danielle; in fact he told them to have a good time.

Mr. Thurmond walked back up to the house and they all got into the boat. Danielle looked at Leed and said, "You go first and I'll drive. Then, Benji can drive while I ski and, I'll drive while he tries out his scoot board, because you aren't driving!"

Leed jumped straight into the water to hide his red face. He had a hard time putting on the bindings in the water; the scoot board was more difficult to get on than the skis were. Leed had to climb out and put them on while sitting on the side of the boat and then jump in. Benji threw him the rope and he tried and tried to get up and stay up but the scoot board just plowed sideways and threw him when he did get almost up.

They stopped and he slipped off the scoot board and they gave him a set of the new skis. After he got them on he was up and skiing in a couple of tries. They went down to the dam, circled and then back up to about the middle of the lake and Leed fell. When they came to throw him the rope he said, "No I've had enough, you go ahead and ski, Danielle."

They changed and took off up the lake and the boys noticed that Danielle, who was good back in the spring, was even better now. She could do long swings to each side and then almost lay down on the water as she turned back toward the other side. Leed admired her beautiful, tanned, shapely body, as she showed them how good a skier she was. Benji took her all the way up to the big basin and made a big turn then brought her all the way back to the dam, before she finally turned loose and they picked her up.

Now it was Benji's turn to test out Leed's invention. His strength, athletic ability and superior balance made him the perfect candidate. He took Leed's advice and got into the bindings on the side of the boat before he jumped into the water. Leed threw Benji the ski rope and, to his surprise, it took Benji three tries before he finally got up. When he did, Danielle took him up the lake and he skied straight for a while, but then he started making slight turns as he got used to it. Soon he was making the long, laying down on the water turns like Danielle. Some of the people in other boats looked kind of funny at Benji as they went by, because they couldn't tell exactly what he was skiing on.

As Benji skied and Danielle drove, Leed kept his eyes on Benji, partly for Benji's safety but mostly so he wouldn't get so tore up looking at Danielle. She was so beautiful, but she was a real business type person like her dad. Leed wanted to ask her out to the drive-in that night, but he just couldn't get up the courage. Finally Benji fell and Danielle picked him up and took them back to the boat dock. As they got out, Leed tried once more to get his courage up, but then she said, "Those scoot boards are a nice invention Leed, you might be able to sell them. I'd like to try skiing on one some day." Leed could only get out a, "Thanks," then Benji cut him off with, "We'll come back one day and let ye try em. See ya Danielle."

Danielle said, "Bye."

Then Leed said, "Bye," as well and waved as she backed away from the dock. He had so wanted to ask her out, but his shyness was too much to overcome.

On the way back home as they were passing the Stone Place, Leed was staring to the right to see if he could see Danielle, when Benji grinned and asked, "Did'ja leave something there?" Leed quickly looked back at the road without answering while his face turned red.

7

BUSINESSMEN

E arly that next week Ronnie and Lonnie made preparation to start the still back up. Before their dad had died, they had soaked corn in a wet toe sack then spread it out to sprout as their dad had told them. Then they ground it and made malt. The malt could be used in the place of yeast to break down the sugars in the corn, to help in the conversion to grain alcohol.

As they carried in the malt, the sacks of ground corn and the bags of sugar to the still house, Ronnie told Lonnie, "We're going to buy yeast from now on, I don't want to make anymore malt It's to much work." They loaded the mash barrels and got everything ready to work off, so they could make a run soon, to start making money. Ronnie had helped his dad do this so much that he was pretty good at it, but Lonnie, who could be amused by about anything, was still to be hollered at by Ronnie just like his dad had to do, so it wasn't much different to him. They went ahead and gathered up enough wood for a run so Lonnie could keep the fire going under the boiler when they cooked off a batch later.

With the hot weather the mash was ready on Friday. Lonnie fired up the still while Ronnie set the 'hydro balance separator'. Lonnie really enjoyed building and tending the fire, and he was good at it. It was the one thing that his dad had spent time teaching him how to do. He didn't know that keeping the fire just right was very important to making liquor. And he didn't know that overheating the mash and sticking it to the still could ruin the still, which was why his dad had worked so hard to teach him. All he knew was that when his daddy showed him how to build a fire and tend it, he talked to him like he had sense, and that was one of the few times that even happened. Lonnie had good thoughts about his dad while he was tending the fire and then he missed him because he had died. Then he remembered all the slappings and he just felt bad. They both worked hard and they worked together and made a good run.

The next day they loaded the huge trunk and back floorboard of their mother's car, like their dad always did, and hauled a load down to Gainesville to the man their dad had dealt with for years. After some talking and sampling of several jars and the assurance from Ronnie that everything that they brought him would be run through the 'hydro balance separator', the man shook hands with both Ronnie and Lonnie and paid them the same price per jar that he always paid their dad.

Ronnie was beaming coming back up the road to the mountains. He and his brother were now businessmen. He looked over at Lonnie and said, "We're businessmen now Lonnie, I think we ought to go out and celebrate tonight. Wha'da'ya thank?"

Lonnie said, "Yeah, we deserve it. Where do you want to go, the drive-in?"

"No," answered Ronnie, "we's men now we ought to go to a beer joint and have a big time."

Lonnie looked puzzled and returned, "But we's only 17 and ya gotta be 21 to drank. We could get arrested in a beer joint."

"I got that figured out," answered Ronnie, "we'll just go out on 76 west of Clayton and go to that beer joint out there, The Fish Bait Inn."

Lonnie, with concern in his voice, asked, "But that's that bad joint where people get cut and shot, ain't it?"

"Don't worry we's men now, they ain't nobody gonna mess with us," a confident Ronnie answered.

They dropped by the house and gave their mom the money from the sale but Ronnie let on like he got only so much and kept a bunch back to honky-tonk with.

As they drove up Bridge Creek Road and turned at Liberty Baptist Church to take the short cut over Davis Gap, Lonnie was getting worried about this venture into the world of men. As they bounced down the other side of the gap and pulled out onto the pavement of highway 76 West, Ronnie started building up his fragile courage by bragging on himself. Soon they pulled into the gravel parking lot and got out and headed for the door.

As they entered they felt uneasy with all the smoke and the rough looking men playing pinball, pool and drinking at the bar and sitting at the tables and booths at the other end of the big room. Ronnie walked over to an opening at the bar and said, "Give me two mugs of brew." The bartender looked at him hard and started to say no, but Ronnie flipped a five on the top of the bar and said, "Keep the change." The bartender grabbed the five and filled two mugs and slid them over to Ronnie. Ronnie handed one to Lonnie and said, "Enjoy." They stood there, feeling out of place, as they sipped their beer. Then Lonnie said, "This stuff tastes awful."

Ronnie knew they stuck out, so he told Lonnie, "Let's get a seat." As they walked toward the only empty booth, Ronnie's elbow bumped the cue stick of one of the men playing pool. The man missed the shot and turned in a rage, cussed Ronnie and flipped his cue stick around intending to hit Ronnie, who ran over toward the wall. There stood Aubrey Denison, the meanest …some say the craziest… man in Rabun County. Ronnie, always a quick thinker, looked at Aubrey and asked, "You want a beer?" Aubrey, knowing what he meant and always lacking money, while looking for a good fight said, "Yeah," and stepped by Ronnie, with his knife already out and open. The man with the cue stick, stopped cold and said, "I don't want no trouble with you, Aubrey." Aubrey just grinned a twisted grin and said, "Well leave my friend alone and they won't be none."

Aubrey joined Ronnie and Lonnie at the booth and the bartender kept them supplied with beer because Ronnie was too afraid to get up and go back to the front so he tipped him well.

As they talked, Ronnie asked Aubrey, "What'cha been up to Aubrey?"

Aubrey answered, "Well I spent some time down in Atlanter working and made pretty good money too, but I blowed it all."

"What'ja blow it on?" asked Ronnie.

"Women," replied Aubrey, with a wild gleam in his eye. Ronnie slid forward with great interest because he couldn't even get a girl to look at him and asked, "How many?"

"As many as you can afford," answered Aubrey, "I found this street that had houses with red porch lights and they's fun places to be."

"I've heard about them," answered Ronnie excitedly, "what was the name of the street?"

"Carol Street, I'll never forget that neither, because two or three of the girls in them houses was named Carol."

Ronnie thought that he would really like to go to Atlanter some day.

After the crowd cleared out, Ronnie and Lonnie left to take Aubrey home because nobody would mess with them while Aubrey was with them. On the way home Lonnie felt safer sitting in the back seat, so he finally asked Aubrey, "You ever been in jail Aubrey?" "Yeah, lots of times, in fact it don't matter how hot I get on a Saturday night, they won't nuttin' cool me off quicker than a good fannin' with a blackjack." Aubrey laughingly answered with a crude attempt at humor.

After dropping Aubrey off, they headed home feeling relieved that they were through trying to prove how tough they were, for now anyway.

Monday when Telford and the boys rolled up in the yard after logging all day, Linda came running out of the house hollering, "It's over! It's over! The war is over!" "What do you mean?" asked Telford. She was still jumping and said, "They announced on the radio that the Korean War just ended and the fightin' is over!" Telford and the boys now joined in with Linda and hugged each other real big because now Larry and Ronald wouldn't be in such danger, and might get to come home soon.

Later that week Telford told the boys, "We need to take the afternoon off and run to town after lunch." When they got through eating, they loaded up and drove through Lakemont, then Wiley and as they got on up the road, Telford looked at the dash of the 1941 Ford pickup and said, "She's gettin' hot boys, we better stop here at Bovard and get some water like the train used to do." They turned off of Highway 441 onto Boggs Mountain Road, crossed the bridge and went about forty yards and stopped.

Telford said, "We better let it cool so we can open the radiator cap."

Benji asked, "Where did the train get its water at, dad?" "Well, they had a water tank up there above the road next to the railroad track back when they used steam trains. And they had a pump down at the creek to pump it up into the wooden tank they had up high so the water would run into the train," answered Telford.

Leed asked, "Why did they decide to put the water station here at Bovard for dad?"

Telford continued, "There's water here and they used up most of what they had on the long pull up to here from Cornelia through Clarkesville, Hollywood, Turnerville and Tallulah Falls, so they had to get water every so often and this was a good spot. The men would come down here next to the road, to this spring, where we're gonna' get water for the truck, and get drinking water, so that was another good reason to stop here." They stood around awhile then walked over to Tiger Creek and looked to see if they could see a trout and threw a few rocks in. Finally their dad took off the radiator cap and filled the radiator with fresh spring water.

They drove on up to Tiger and stopped at Roane's store, just past the Texaco station and went inside. Telford said, "Boys, ya'll been working hard, get a snack and a drank, I'll cover it!" They both went up and down the candy isle and they both stopped and looked at a package of Pinwheels. They held them up and asked their dad if they were OK. He said, "Sure!" Then they each went and got a Coca-Cola® and opened them on the side of the ice box, went up to the register and Telford paid. As they went outside, they both turned their Cokes up and killed them straight down, like a Coke ought to be drunk. Leed thought how refreshing that was. Then they both went back in and got their deposit back and gave it to their dad.

As they drove on toward town, they opened the Pinwheels and enjoyed the chocolate outer layer, the marshmallow inner part and the cookie that it was sitting on. They both had that look of enjoyment on their faces as those Pinwheels kept melting in their mouths.

They went on to town and went to the Western Auto Store and got a part for their chain saw then headed back home.

The next Saturday Leed and Benji went back to the Lake Rabun Boat Dock to 'look' around. As Leed got out of the truck on the other side of the road, he saw Danielle, standing about halfway down the steps that led to the store on the docks, talking to another girl. He quickly crossed the road and got to Danielle just as the conversation was ending. He got his courage up and said, "Hello Danielle how are you?" "Oh fine," she answered and started walking on down the steps. Leed determined not to let her get away, followed and kept talking and she talked with him as they walked down along the dock by the water, to the place where people could eat on the tables and benches. They sat down, still talking.

Leed was excited because things were going so well and he asked her about skiing and swimming. He was getting his courage up to ask her out to the drive-in that night when another boy walked up and said, "Hey, Danielle, are you ready to go?" She answered, "Yes, but first I want you to meet Leed Brown a local boy. Leed, this is Keith Warren." They shook hands and exchanged greetings, and then Keith and Danielle left with only a, "Bye," from Danielle. Leed felt so stupid that he had finally stuck his neck out to talk with a girl and she was only waiting on her boyfriend. He knew it would be a long time before he could talk to a girl again.

The next week Leed was lonelier than ever and on Saturday night Benji and Tommy Hawk went to the drive-in with cousin Ray, but Leed told them that he just didn't feel like going and stayed at home. Telford and Linda were down at Bill and Gertrude's doing the bobby pin thing, so Leed was by himself. He was so lonely that he walked all the way around the side of the mountain to the low cliffs and just sat there and thought about how he would soon start his senior year in high school and he didn't know what he would do after that. His grades were good enough to get him into most any college, but money was real scarce for honest folks in these mountains and he knew his mom and dad didn't have the money to send him to college.

He didn't mind going to work after high school but he didn't even have a girl to share life with either and that really made his heart heavy. As he sat there thinking, a lonely Whippoorwill started whistling in the trees to the right of the cliff. Soon another Whippoorwill answered the first; it was to the left and behind Leed. They were so close that Leed could clearly hear the click that they make just as they started their 'Whip-poor-will' whistle. This exchange was beautiful; but it was so lonely that it pulled Leed's sprit down even lower. He wished so hard for a girl and to have a chance to prove himself in college. With his head hung low he realized how tough life really is. Then he thought about Jesus and how lonely it must have been on the cross. He wondered why Jesus even went to the cross. "Was it to save people, maybe even, me?" Leed sat there thinking until late that night, there was a lot on his young mind.

8 WARWOMAN

The next three weeks were real busy. Their dad had bought up a stand of pines from the government, down off of Warwoman Road. The stand was way up Sarah's Creek, back through Apple Valley, and over in on Walnut Fork Creek on the Warwoman Refuge. They moved the mules down there and enough feed so they could leave them in a pen they built for the duration of the job. They worked six days a week to get the timber out and up to Ritter's Saw Mill. The Warwoman area was rough, and some of the pines they were logging were up on a shelf and had to be brought down off of a rough side to the loading yard, next to the road. The pines on the shelf were also big and they had to use both of their mules, Ben and Maud, to pull them. The pair had been raised and trained by grandpa and were good alone, but they could really pull a big load when they were hooked together onto a doubletree.

As they were clearing a drag trail down the rough side, Telford told Leed and Benji, "Boys, this is the kind of place where the logs can ball-hoot and catch up with the mules. That's how men and mules get killed, so we had better fix the mules a cut-out."

"What's a cut-out dad?" asked Benji.

Telford explained, "Well son that's a opening off to one side of the drag trail that the mules can jump out into if the log ball-hoots."

"Won't the logs and chain just drag them on down the hill anyway?" asked Benji. "No your grandpa taught them to not only jump over into the cut-out, but to hunker down right then and lean into the harness hard in anticipation of the logs going by and the chain getting tight. The J grabs are designed to knock out sideways and pull out sideways, too. So they jerk the J grabs out and let the logs go on 'til they stop," said Telford.

"That's good! I'd hate to lose one of the mules," finished Benji.

Their dad had a big McCullough 5-49, two-man bow-saw that they used to fell the big trees and saw them up. Leed and Benji both marveled how their dad could wield the big two man saw by himself, but most of the time when they were cutting logs, Benji teamed with his dad and manned the other end of the saw. Leed's job when the log hit the ground was to take the big double bit axe and take the limbs off. His dad had taught him how to stick one side of the axe in a stump and then file straight down on both sharp edges to put a knife like edge on the axe. He would then flip it over and do the same on the other side. He liked using the axe; there was a lot of physics involved in logging and using the axe was no exception. His dad had taught him to hit the base of the limb in close to the log. If he caught it just right, even a big white pine limb would just jump off the tree on the first lick. If not he would change the angle and take a big chip out and get the limb with one or two more licks.

———————————

On Thursday night of the first week Telford told the boys that they were going to spend the weekend down on Warwoman where the mules were. So they packed food, frying pans, utensils, a coffee pot, boilers, quilts and an old tarp that was in the barn. The next morning they stopped by Roane's store and bought a whole case of Cokes to take with them. They carried all of it down to the level spot by the branch where the mules were. They placed the case of Cokes, jug of milk and the eggs in the branch to stay cold and set up camp. Then they worked all day logging.

That evening they drove around to Walnut Fork and walked about a hundred yards up an old road along the little creek to take a bath in the creek. Their dad showed them two holes that were each bigger than two big wash tubs that the creek had eroded out in solid rock just below the road. One was mostly full of sand and rocks but the water washed in a fast circle in the other and it was about thigh deep. Warwoman Refuge covers the southeast flank of Rabun Bald and this water comes right out of the base of Rabun Bald, the second highest mountain in the state of Georgia. It was very cold, not having been out of the ground long.

When they got into this tub for their evening bath they didn't even stay in the water as long as they did at Stonewall Falls, because this water was even colder. In fact, Benji tried to see how long he could stay hunkered down to his neck after Telford and Leed had bathed. When he finally stood up after about three minutes he had to be helped out because his legs would hardly function. They handed him a towel and he stood there and shook for awhile before he could walk to the truck even though it was very warm.

On Saturday they worked 'till late morning and Telford told the boys that they were going to do something special. They went back to camp and loaded his old army pack with supplies. Then he said, "We're going to hike all the way up the Rabun Bald Trail to the top of Rabun Bald and spend the night there tonight. In the morning we'll see the sunrise."

They drove to where the trail crossed the road and started the long hike to the top of Rabun Bald. They stopped at where water sprang out of the ground, just a few hundred yards from the top and got some to drink and cook with. Then they walked on up to the top of the mountain and set up camp right by the rock based fire tower. There was no Forest Ranger there watching for fire, because it had rained regularly that summer and the woods weren't dry.

Rabun Bald was called bald because being almost 4,700 feet above sea level, it had ice on top many mornings way on up into May or June. This stunted the trees so much that none of them were over fifteen or twenty feet tall. That was the reason the fire tower was only about fifteen feet high to the lookout floor.

They fixed supper quickly and ate just before dark, then hurried and laid out their quilt beds because they hadn't brought a lantern. They were in awe at God's creation as they lay there looking up at the stars that filled the sky. No one said a word as the stars grew brighter and brighter in the large expanse of sky that was available to them on this mountaintop, thanks to the short trees. Leed even thought of the order in the universe and how it pointed at a Great Designer.

The next morning Telford got up early and walked down to the spring to get coffee water, water for grits and the eggs out of the spring. He walked back up and gathered more wood and made breakfast over the fire he built among the little cooking rocks. Leed thought about how good a father he had in Telford and how his close relationship with the Lord was what made the difference in this mountain man.

After breakfast Telford reached in his pack and pulled out his Bible and they all sat down on the ground, and as the sun was coming up over the ridges back in South Carolina, he read all thirty-one verses of Genesis, Chapter 1 and the first three verses of Genesis, Chapter 2. Then he turned over to Colossians, Chapter 1 and verses thirteen through sixteen. "Boys, here the Bible tells us that Jesus Christ created what He talked about in Genesis and that includes everything that you see from this lofty perch." Then he read, "'Who hath delivered us from the power of darkness, and hath translated us into the kingdom of his dear Son: In Whom we have redemption through His blood, even the forgiveness of sins: Who is the image of the invisible God, the Firstborn of every creature: For by Him were all things created that are in heaven, and that are in earth, visible and invisible, whether they be thrones, or dominions, or principalities, or powers: all things were created by Him and for Him:'"

Telford closed his Bible and bowed his head and thanked the Lord for the great creation, then he told them to think about the Bible reading for awhile. Afterward they talked and just rested and enjoyed the view for awhile. Rabun Bald was so high that when they looked down toward Dillard and Rabun Gap, it was like looking down on a map. You could see the roads and the small looking buildings but the three dimensional relief of this map was so very beautiful.

Leed and Benji climbed up on the tower and walked around the narrow porch looking into North Carolina, South Carolina and a large portion of Rabun County. Looking to the southeast they could see a cliff and Benji asked Telford what it was called. He said,

"Salt Rock which is on the north side of Marsen Knob, which is part of the mountain range that Black Rock Mountain is on. In fact you see right there where U.S. Highway 441 runs just to the left of Marsen Knob, well that's where Ritter's Sawmill is."

Soon Telford said they had better go down and check on the mules. Leed and Benji reluctantly started their hike down off the top of Rabun Bald, their latest favorite new place in Rabun County.

Monday they worked and then went home for the first time since Friday morning. They were all glad to see Linda and especially her home cooking. After the camping trip and with all of the work, the boys were too tired to do anything but sleep at night and go to church on Sunday, the only day they had off. Finally they finished the stand and got the mules moved back to the farm on Saturday of the third week. The next day they went to church that morning and then everyone was looking forward to the big singing Sunday night.

That night they got to church early to get a good seat because they expected a crowd; the Loundes Family and Sister McCray were coming to sing. The Loundes family traveled all around singing hymns and gospel music. Sister McCray was a blind lady who loved the Lord and who also loved to sing. When she sang about her Lord and Savior Jesus Christ, she would get so loud and so high they say she blew the globes around some lights out, in a church over in South Carolina, one time. Everyone had a great time, especially Leed who greatly enjoyed Sister McCray and her enthusiasm. On the way home he thought that he would like to be close to the Lord like Sister McCray, but she was a real special person who served the Lord all of the time, not just a regular person like he was. These thoughts stayed with Leed until sleep came late that night.

On Monday, right after breakfast, Linda told Leed and Benji,

"I missed you boys while ya'll were down on Warwoman, I had to draw water by myself when I washed clothes! Since Telford's gonna' let y'all lay off a logging this week, then I need your help. There's a big pile of clothes that I didn't even wash a waitin', as well as some of both of yun's school clothes that I got out of a box that need washed before school starts back next week. So if ya'll will get to drawing water and filling up both big wash tubs, we'll get started!"

She walked out on the porch and rolled the old Maytag wringer washer over to the edge of the porch against the banister and went to get the washing powders and clothes. Leed went over to a shelf on the wall and got a screw-in plug adapter, then a chair and climbed up on the chair and unscrewed the porch light from the holder that was hanging down by the twisted pair of braided wires that were feeding it. He then held the bulb holder and screwed in the plug-in adapter. He climbed down and put the bulb on the shelf, went to the washing machine, got the washer plug-in and climbed back up on the chair. He plugged up the washer and pulled the string to turn on the porch light holder so the washer would run then climbed down and put the chair back against the wall.

While Leed was plugging up the washer, Benji went to the well, which was built into the porch, at the end where the meat house was. He picked up the well bucket, flipped the wooden lid back on the well and dropped the well bucket in the black hole. The well bucket was tied to a rope that went up over a pulley that was hung on a porch rafter. The rope then went back down and wrapped around a smooth log windlass, about three feet long, that had a three-quarter inch rod that had been pushed through it by repeatedly heating the rod and burning a hole through the center of it years ago. To keep the windlass from slipping on the rod, two straps of metal were clamped around the rod and nailed to the end of the log. The three-quarter inch rod stuck out the far end about six inches and laid in between two blocks of wood with some old shoe leather for bearings. The near side stuck through a similar bearing block also, before it made two ninety-degree bends and ended as a ten inch offset handle.

The well was about forty five feet deep, so as the bucket fell faster and faster the log windlass and metal rod handle were spinning so fast that they were about to lift the top off of the old bearing blocks. When it hit the water, it stopped but the windlass kept on spinning until the rope was all off down to the nails that held it on, then it wrapped up about four turns of rope backwards and stopped. Benji jerked the rope a couple of times until he felt the well bucket had enough water in it, then he picked up on the rope and chugged the well bucket straight down so it would sink and fill up. He then started turning the handle of the windlass to bring the now heavy bucket back up to the top.

The boys had performed this job ever since their oldest brother Larry had gone into the Army and the next brother Ronald had gone into the Marines, so they were very mechanical in their methods. When the bucket came out of the well opening, Leed was waiting and caught the handle with his left hand and the bottom with his right hand and headed for the wash tub, by the washing machine about fifteen feet away. Benji gave the windlass handle a flip backwards, as he turned it loose to give Leed the slack he needed to walk swiftly to the wash tub. Leed poured the water into the tub in a flash, but he had learned to pour it straight down to keep from splashing it out. As Leed walked back Benji winched up the slack in the rope so the bucket wouldn't jerk the rope too hard when Leed dropped it into the well.

Linda's youngest two sons stayed hard at filling up the first wash tub as she loaded the washer with clothes and washing powders then started dipping the water into the washer with a long handled boiler.

Leed would pour well buckets full of water directly into the washer when she needed it. They would get both of the tubs full and go to loafing, but as soon as Linda got one tub out and started on the second tub she would call them back to their job.

When she went in to fix lunch she told Leed to wring out a load for her. He walked over and turned the agitator lever off, removed the lid and picked up the drain pipe, with the curved end, that hung on the side of the washer to keep the water in and dropped it through the porch railings to drain the dirty water. Then he flipped another lever to engage the wringer. His next task was to pick up the wet clothes out of the washer, spread them out and run them through the wringer that was made up of two, rubber coated rollers driven through a small gearbox on a swivel on one side of the washer. When not in use it could be swung out of the way. But Leed

70

had it over the washer, where the water from the wet clothes ran down a tray and into the washer. As the clean clothes ran through the wringer he would catch them and place them in a basket.

Leed was worried enough that someone might see him helping out with the washing or running the washing machine; he sure didn't want to go out in the open and hang clothes out where he almost for sure would get caught, so he left the basket of clothes for his mom. She could hang them out on the clothesline. They worked hard till afternoon when she finally told them the water they had in the two tubs was enough to finish.

9

BACK TO SCHOOL

L ater that week on Thursday, Leed spoke to his dad, "We been working hard and school starts real soon. We want to get Tommy Hawk and go down to the big river and swim over on the South Carolina side, there at Bull Sluice. Is that OK?" Telford smiled and said, "Sure, you both have been working real hard and that ought to be fun. Just be careful."

They put on their cut off jeans then went to Tommy Hawk's. He put on his cut off jeans as well and they headed out. Instead of going all the way to town and back down U.S. 76, they just cut through Wolf Creek Road which ran down by Cutting Bone Creek, where Cindy Lewis lived with her mom and grandma. They continued on down across the lower end of Stekoa Creek and on out to U.S. 76, not too far from the South Carolina bridge.

They drove down to the line, which was the Chattooga River and across the bridge, then turned left down a little old road that led a couple of hundred yards up the river on the South Carolina side. They parked and jumped out and ran all the way to the sand bar just below Bull Sluice. Bull Sluice was a rock outcropping that crossed from Georgia to South Carolina and the whole river poured over it into a deep channel. The sand bar led out near this channel and the river wasn't very wide here.

Most of the water poured over the lower side of the outcropping on the Georgia side and only a small smooth layer of water poured over the long, almost level rolling edge of the outcropping on the South Carolina side. They all went for the outcropping on the South Carolina side because over the years rocks had gotten

74

into small depressions on the top edge of the outcropping and had been washed around and around until they made a couple of perfect round holes down into the rock that were full of water.

The holes were hard to find, with the thin layer of water pouring over the outcropping at a good speed. The boys were all scooting along the edge, hunting the holes, because only one hole was big enough to get all the way down in. In fact you could hold your breath and disappear down into the hole under the thin layer of water pouring over the outcropping. This looked strange from the sandbar.

Benji found the deep hole and slid down into it, then came right back out and hollered, "There's something in there!"

Leed, as he scooted up to the hole asked, "What did it feel like?"

"I guess it was a bunch of little fish, why?" answered Benji.

"Well I didn't want to get on no snake!" said Leed, as he smiled and slid into the hole. He went all the way down in the hole completely under water. As the cool water and low roar of the river going over the sluice surrounded him, he thought, "This feels like being inside a barrel full of water and it's about the same size."

About that time he felt a hand on the top of his head holding him down, and he knew that Benji was getting him back for sliding into the hole that he had found. Leed stood up with all of his might and rose up out of the hole. His brother tried to jump in with him but couldn't get all the way in. Leed said, "Wait, I'll get out, you can have it, just get off of me!"

Benji backed up and Leed got out and gave him the hole and just sat on the outcropping as the thin layer of water went around him and over the edge. He put his hands behind him, letting his feet hang over the outcrop, leaned back and allowed the sun to shine on him. Soon Tommy Hawk slid in beside him and did the same. Leed looked at him and said, "This cool water feels good after three weeks of hard work logging up where some of this water comes from?"

Tommy grinned and said, "Yeah, we better enjoy, school starts back next week."

After a while on the outcropping, Leed and Tommy Hawk slid

down onto the rocks below and crossed through the still water to the sandbar. But the daring Benji walked out to the edge of the sluice and just jumped right into the swift white water, grabbing his knees as he rode it out. In a couple of seconds he bobbed up in the swift water and started swimming hard toward the sandbar. The swift water was too much and he came out down stream, about thirty yards, and then walked back up to where Leed and Tommy Hawk were.

They lay around in the sun and swam some more, not wanting this last bit of freedom to end before school started the next week. But finally they dried a while and headed for the truck and home.

This was the last weekend before school started and some guys were coming over to the house to play bluegrass before the boys went back to the books. This was not a big get together like the Fourth of July, just some of Telford's friends and family that had a pretty serious band. They were going to practice and work on some new songs that they were adding to their list. Leed really liked this, since they weren't showing out and got real serious about their music. They even did one shape note song, they started out singing their parts in shape notes, that's doe, ray me, fa, so, la, etc. then after one time through they sung 'In That Morning' with words using the same notes as before. It was beautiful, he thought. They picked and sang until pretty late, and then four of them stood up and slid their guitars and mandolin around on their backs and laid the banjo down and sang several gospel songs without any instruments.

Their harmony and the words they were singing about their Lord affected Leed in a powerful way, but it also made him feel funny because he didn't know what to do about it. After everyone had gone and he was laying in bed that night he drifted off to sleep thinking of the words, "Going up home to live in green pastures," and, "Deep settled peace," and the words that haunted him most, "What would you give, in exchange for your soul?"

The next week school started back and the guys were all talking about their summers. Furlon Stancil was older than the rest of the boys because of a couple of trips through some of the same grades, so he was kind of a leader of, but not the best influence on the boys Leed's age. After everyone left but Furlon and Leed, he asked Leed, "Did you get you a girlfriend this summer?" Leed, needing someone to talk to, opened up to Furlon about Danielle and his frustration. Furlon said, "You got to quit being so soft on these girls, they like a man who knows what he wants and not some sissy that beats around the bush. Why don't you ask Betty Dewbury out to the drive-in Friday night?" Leed answered, "Well, I guess I could." Furlon shot back, "You ain't afraid to ask her out are ye?" Leed answered, "No." "Well, now when you get to the drive-in you have to show her you mean business. As soon as it gets dark you look straight at her and tell her to get in the back seat, you got it?" "Yeah," answered Leed.

Thursday Leed mustered his courage and started talking to Betty Dewbury, soon he felt comfortable and asked her out to the drive-in on Friday night and she said yes. He was surprised how well things worked, Furlon's way.

That night he asked his dad and mom to borrow the car to take Betty out to the drive-in the next night. His mom got that very concerned look in her eye and asked, "When did you start liking her?" Leed said, "We just started talking today." "Well, we don't know her folks all that well and this kind'a concerns me," answered his mom.

"Aw, it's just one date mom."

His mother in her wisdom then stated, "Son, every date is a potential marriage partner." They finally agreed to loan him the car and Leed slipped off to the bedroom. Benji came in after a few minutes and started getting ready for bed.

He looked over at Leed, who was already in bed and asked, "You goin' out with Betty Dewbury? That thangs as dumb as a brick." Then he shook his head and got in bed.

Leed got to thinking, Betty wasn't all that smart for sure but she was fairly good looking and she seemed to really like it when Leed talked to her and he liked it when she paid attention back, smiling and blinking her eyes funny when she looked at him; he was going through with it anyway, even if it was a little questionable.

The next night Leed picked Betty up late, so he could pull this off under the cover of darkness. He drove to the drive-in, paid and parked off to one side. He was nervous, it was almost dark and the movie was starting. Leed, with his heart pounding, finally got his courage up and looked straight at Betty and said, "Get in the back seat!" Betty gave him a puzzled look, that turned to hurt and then, with tears starting to form, she replied, "I, I don't want to get in the back seat, I want to stay up here with you." Then she put her head in her hands and cried. Leed tried to say something but all he could get out was, "But a-a-a."

Betty raised her head and looked straight at Leed and said, "If you're ashamed of me and don't want to be seen with me settin' next to you, then you can just take me home. Right now!"

Leed finally got out an, "OK."

After Leed took her home he was too ashamed to go home so early, so he drove up to Clayton and drove through town a couple of times. He finally saw some guys he knew parked down by the train tracks where Chechero Road starts, and he pulled in and got out to stand around and talk with them. After a while it started sprinkling rain, so one of the guys whose name was Slim Nations asked Leed if he wanted to ride around with him for a while. Leed said, "Yeah," even though Slim's old car looked pretty bad. Slim looked at the gas gauge and said, "Better get some gas," so they drove up to the Standard station on Main Street and Slim put in 50¢ worth of gas, before taking off down Warwoman Road with Slim driving hard. After they rode all the way down to Highway 28, at Pine Mountain, Slim turned around and drove all the way back up Warwoman Road to town where he put in 50¢ worth of gas again. Leed overcome with curiosity asked, "Why just 50¢ worth at a time Slim."

Slim came right back with, "This thang could tear up at any time and leave all that money a settin' on the side of the road in the gas tank, I ain't a gonna do it!"

After getting gas they rode down by Leed's car and went all the way down Chechero Road to the South Carolina line where Slim turned around just before the bridge and headed back to town. It was still raining and it was getting late, so Leed just slid his shoes off and pulled his knees up to his chest, slid around sideways with his back to the door and his sock feet on the seat and laid his head over against the back of the seat and dozed off to the slapping of the windshield wipers. Slim was still driving hard and fast as they came up the stretch by the Kingwood Mansion and started up the mountain heading into town.

In a long curve near the top of the mountain the slick tires lost traction and Slim lost control of the car. They started sliding completely sideways around the curve and up the hill. Slim freaked out as he looked out the drivers side window at two cars coming straight at them. He left his driving position and jumped in the back seat, wrapped his arms around the part of the seat that you sit on and screamed, "We'er killed!" The scream woke Leed, into an unfolding nightmare. Because of the shock of being awakened so suddenly, he couldn't move a muscle, but he was conscious of every thing that was going on. For Leed everything seemed to be happening in slow motion. The car was sliding up the road sideways, the headlights of two cars were heading straight at the drivers side door, shining straight into Leed's eyes, and Slim was squalling like a baby while still wrapped around the back seat. In what seemed like an eternity, the two on-coming cars came to a stop a safe distance from the driver's door, and Slim's car finally slid to a stop cross-ways in the middle of the road.

Then the car, still in high gear with the motor now dead, started chugging forward toward the right side of the road, because the road was banked hard to the right for the curve. The car was heading for a very deep hole that was all grown up in Kudzu and all Leed had to do was reach his foot over and mash the brake to stop it. But he was still completely frozen after being awakened by the scream, and was unable to force his body to do anything. Slim was still clutching the back seat slobbering and crying. The car was moving faster now and Leed was trying harder to make his body work, but to no avail. The car rolled right off the pavement with a slight jar as Leed desperately tried to activate his terror-frozen body. Then the car slowly rolled over the edge, in dream like fashion, and tumbled end over end twice. Stark reality returned quickly and they ended up at the bottom of the hole with the grille stuck into the branch. One car from above went for the Sheriff, and the other man came down and helped Slim and Leed out of the hole. Both were beat up pretty good but were able to climb out. After the Deputy got there and checked them out he took them to the new Rabun County Hospital where they were cleaned up and bandaged. The Deputy took Leed back to his car and Slim on home without charging him with anything because of the wet roads.

When Leed got home his mom, who had keen interest in this date he had been on, was waiting up for him. She was pretty rattled when she saw him. She asked, "What did ya'll do?" Then she asked how he was and checked out the bandages. He explained what had happened, and she said, "I won't wake your dad now, but you need to have a good talk with him tomorrow!" His mom just stared at him, shaking her head, but he looked tired and hurt so she told him to go on to bed.

The next morning a very sore Leed got out of bed and came to the kitchen, just as his mom was setting breakfast on the table. His dad said, "Let's bow our heads," and he prayed, "Father, thank You for bringing my son home alive last night, and thank You for the lessons he learned about going out and doing things on his on, without talking them over with You, or me. I ask that You would use this to draw him to Yourself and to help him to mature. Also Father, thank You for this food, we ask that You would use it to nourish our bodies. I ask these things in the name of Jesus Christ my Lord and my Love, Amen."

Everyone ate in silence. After breakfast, Telford helped Linda clean the table which was a rare sight, he normally only did that when he had that gleam in his eye and wanted to hug that beautiful woman in the apron. Leed was out on the porch setting in the swing when his dad walked out and sat down beside him. Telford looked at him and said, "Son you're almost a man now and probably the smartest man I know, and that includes your grandpa. But you gotta' learn to use them smarts to get through life. Like when your momma don't think something's right, then it probably ain't right, and you gotta' learn that you don't get in the car with Slim Nations when he's been drinking or not, even a little. And most of all, you gotta' notice that God has put His whole creation around you to point you to Him, and He's doing a lot of other things in your life right now to get your attention, and you ain't pay'en Him no attention!" Leed thought, "Could God really want my attention? Why, I've done so many stupid things that there's no way He would want to know me?"

His dad, noticing Leed's lack of attention said, "Are you listening to me, son?"

Leed stuttered, "Yes… yes, dad, I was just thinking about what you was saying."

Telford closed with, "Well, I want you to keep thinking about what I just told you, OK." Leed agreed and looking straight into his dad's firm but loving eyes, said, "Thanks dad."

A tear came to Telford's eye as he put his arm around Leed and said, "I love you son." And they both hugged for a long minute.

The next day at church Leed tried to pay attention to Preacher Bill's sermon, but his dad's challenge was being met in his head at the same time, as he thought about what Telford had said. Then Preacher Bill got to preaching in Romans again and some verses broke through to Leed. He noticed that in chapter 1 and verse 18, he read about how bad Leed was, and in verses 19 and 20 he read about the creation, pointing to God, like his dad had talked about. Then in the following verses, he read about how men who reject God think that they are wise, but aren't and how they end up worshipping themselves and then, God gives them up. Leed thought about how he was doing that in his own head and then he got scared and thought about how he didn't want to reject God, but how could he have a relationship with God when he was just a man so far from God. He just couldn't figure out how to get to God.

After the service was over Leed was sore, stiff and exhausted, so he went out and sat in the car while everyone talked and finally they went home. Leed would be glad when he could go back to school the next day. He liked books and studying.

The next day at school Leed didn't spend any time in the hall-way, because he was afraid he might have to face Betty Dewbury and he wasn't looking forward to that. Ronnie and Lonnie walked around school like they were too big to be there, and with their big bellies, they were about right.

That night Ronnie and Lonnie with Jeff, Lonnie's faithful dog and only friend, headed out behind the barn and up the ridge to the government land where the still was, to get ready for a run. They poured the mash from the barrels into the still with buckets, then Lonnie built a fire under the boiler. Ronnie was filling the 'hydro balance separator' up on one side with water to get it ready for the run when Jeff growled. Ronnie looked at Lonnie and asked, "What's he growling at?"

Lonnie answered, "I don't know, but I thank I see a light coming up though the woods way down yonder."

Ronnie whispered right loud, "Revenourers, run!" Lonnie and Jeff took off around the side of the hill, while Ronnie stepped up, grabbed the 'hydro balance separator', jerked the lines loose from it and took off, angling up the ridge above where Lonnie and Jeff had just gone. Lonnie and Jeff went way around Crumley Mountain and finally stopped to listen and see if anyone was following them.

After listening a few seconds, Lonnie heard someone running around the mountain above them. He looked down at Jeff and said, "C'mon Jeff, Ronnie's right up yonder." They started up the mountain to meet up with Ronnie and as they got closer, Jeff could hear Ronnie real well by now, so he ran up the hill and fell in on the trail following him. But Ronnie didn't know that it was Jeff; he thought it was the revenuers chasing him, so he took off. Ronnie ran and Jeff followed. Ronnie ran farther, and Jeff stayed faithfully behind him the whole way. Ronnie finally reached complete exhaustion and couldn't go any more. He staggered a few more steps and fell over, still clutching the 'hydro balance separator' to his chest, breathing giant gulps of air and knowing that he was caught and

82

going to jail. About that time Jeff walked up right above him and laid down, panting with his tongue hanging out.

By the faint moon light Ronnie saw and realized it was Jeff and not a revenuer, so he just continued to gulp air and never released his grip on the 'hydro balance separator'. After awhile Lonnie caught up and said, "Boy we shore did out run them revenuers, didn't we?" Ronnie, finally getting his breath said, "I'm gonna kill that dog; he liked to have run me to death." Lonnie answered, with great concern for his friend, Jeff, "No you ain't. Me and him is gitt'n out'a here!" and they took off down the holler and slept in a thicket on the leaves until morning, when they slipped home about the same time as Ronnie. As they were going into the house Ronnie said, "We better stop for awhile till things cool down. We can spend the time get'n a new still built." Lonnie said "OK." About a week later they slipped up to the secret site and looked at their still. It was chopped to pieces along with the barrels and even several feet of the water pipe hadn't been spared. They slipped away knowing that they had to find a new, safer site before starting back in business.

10 FOOTBALL

That week Telford told the boys, "The field corn is dry enough to cut the fodder tops. I'll cut 'em during the day and when ya'll get in from school, ya'll can put them in the dry for feed this winter." Fodder tops, being the blades of the corn stalk pulled up and together, tied off and cut, were easier to put up than hay because they were light. But still, as much as their dad planned to cut, would take a couple of evenings to haul and pack tight together in the barn.

Friday after school, with a few tops still to put in the barn, Benji was getting nervous. Leed hurried with him and got them in the barn real quick. Then they headed to the house to clean up. Tonight was the first football game of the season and Benji really wanted to go. He was faster and stronger than any of the boys on the team and the year before, when they had started football at Rabun County High School, the coach had asked him to play. But Telford had said no, he needed him and Leed to load logs so they could make a living. The coach tried again this year to get Benji to play, but to no avail even though Benji yearned to play.

They drove up to Clayton and parked up next to the courthouse like their dad told them, so the car wouldn't get scratched. As they walked across the street and down the sidewalk toward the gym, the crowd was already filing in. Rabun County High School started playing football just the year before but the team was well supported on Friday night.

Down at the field they found a spot by the cable that was strung to keep the crowd back. In a little while several other boys had joined Leed and Benji and they were all talking and acting bigger than they really were. All of a sudden Leed spotted Betty Dewbury and two other girls approaching the crowd of boys. He swallowed hard and turned into the crowd to keep from making eye contact. After she went by, he watched where she went so he could stay away from her the rest of the night.

Soon the kickoff came and the crowd really got into it. But Leed could tell it was almost torture for Benji to stand there while all the action was out on the field. When people ran, Benji would make little turning motions, like he was running with them, and when they hit, he would stiffen at the sound. Football was a lot of fun to watch, but Leed also enjoyed watching everyone in the bleachers and standing along the cable having a good time. It was amazing how much emotion people showed, and it was just a game.

The night was fairly warm and Benji had expended so much energy, running while standing and hitting in his mind, that he was soon sweating like one of the players.

When the game was over, Leed and Benji walked fast through the crowd, and as they got up toward the court house, Benji said, "I wish I could play with them boys!" Leed knew that being raised in the mountains was tough on both of them. They both had dreams that life in the mountains just didn't provide for.

———————————

On Saturday, Ronnie and Lonnie didn't have anything to do so Ronnie said, "I got an idea on how to show everybody how smart we are and how big a men we are."

"What's that?" asked Lonnie.

"I'll tell you on the way," then they went in and Ronnie asked his mom, "Can we borrow your car to go to town?"

She said, "You better not wreck it up!"

"I won't," answered Ronnie. When they were outside Ronnie told Lonnie, "You got to leave that dog here!"

"But Jeff wants to go. See? Look at him."

"No," I said, "now get in!" ordered Ronnie.

Lonnie looked at Jeff and said, "Bye my buddy, we'll be back later, you go and rest and don't be chasin' no chickens or mama's gonna' shoot ye!"

As they drove Lonnie asked, "What are we going to do?"

"We're going to catch Slewfoot!" beamed Ronnie. Lonnie, who was afraid of Slewfoot, asked with wide-eyed apprehension, "How?"

"We're going to the trash dump and lure him into the trunk of the car with pieces of that bread I stole out of the kitchen," answered Ronnie, still beaming over his idea.

"I'm skeered," whined Lonnie, "let's don't do it."

"Aw it'll be easy," countered Ronnie. They drove up the hill to the trash dump and sure enough, there was Slewfoot digging in the garbage with no fear of the boys as they pulled over and backed the car up the hill toward where he was pawing. Ronnie stopped the car a good distance away and got out. He had to go to the other side and drag a trembling Lonnie out.

Then he raised the lid on the big trunk of his mama's car and told Lonnie, "You get on top of the car and hide behind the trunk where Slewfoot can't see you, and when I lure him into the trunk with this bread, you slam the lid down and we'll have him." Lonnie glad to be out of sight, climbed right up on the car.

After throwing bread toward the bear from a safe distance, then leaving a trail of bread pieces up to the trunk of the car, Ronnie baited the trunk with several, more pieces. Then he slipped over to the edge of the woods and stood behind a scrub pine to watch. After eating the first piece, Slewfoot ate his way quickly up to the car. Once he had devoured the bread on the ground, he placed his feet on the bumper and looked into the trunk where more bread waited. His weight moved the car and Lonnie was about to cry, but Ronnie settled him down with a hand motion and then mouthed, "Get ready." With only slight hesitation, Slewfoot climbed right over into the trunk and started gobbling the last of the bread. Ronnie motioned to Lonnie to slam the lid down. As Lonnie leaned forward and pushed the trunk lid to close it, he lost his footing and slid down over the trunk slamming the big heavy lid hard over the huge bear. Slewfoot was theirs.

Ronnie came running, whooping and hollering, as Lonnie got

up off the ground. Then he joined in on the celebration with a very 'get down' dance routine around behind the car. But about that time, the car lurched back and forth as an angry Slewfoot started moving around, searching for a way out. As the bear became more aggravated, the boys heard the sound of metal crunching and Lonnie's victory dance turned into contortions of shock.

Then to Ronnie's amazement, Slewfoot ripped through the back seat with springs pinging and popping and cloth ripping. He tore the headliner and the back of the front seat to shreds with just a couple swipes of his massive paw. He reached up with one paw and broke the back of the front seat and laid it down flat. He moved up to the steering wheel and stuck his huge head out the driver's side window and looked back at Ronnie and Lonnie who were standing, rooted in place out of shock and fear. In all the commotion, he knocked the car out of gear and it started rolling down the hill, faster and faster while Slewfoot continued to look back at Ronnie and Lonnie. Finally, as the car rolled out of sight, Lonnie exclaimed, "Slewfoot just stole mama's car!" Ronnie fretted, "Mama's gonna kill us!"

Lonnie looked at him and said, "It weren't my idea!"

They walked down the hill and finally found the car, smashed into a tree with the driver's side door torn about half off. They caught a ride home, where Ronnie began to tell their mama what happened. Before he could even finish, she said, "I'll take this outta yer hides!" and went to find her a stick. They used the opportunity to slip out and hide in the barn loft until the next day, when they got hungry. When they finally came in the house she looked real mean at them and said, "You boys is gonna' walk from now on cause ye ain't got sense enough to drive."

That next Friday night Leed and Benji gathered around the radio with their dad, as they did regular, waitin' for the Friday Night Fights to come on. They talked about Rocky Marciano the World Heavyweight Champion. The Champ had already knocked out 'Jersey' Joe Walcott in the spring and on the radio they were talking about how he had knocked out Roland LaStarza just the night before, meaning he was still the undefeated Heavyweight Champion of the world. This was one of the most popular shows on the radio, and one of Telford's and the boy's favorites also. Telford really liked boxing. He had boxed real well while he was in the Army, he had often told the boys. Sometimes before the fights came on, he would take the boys out into the yard and show them how to stand, crouch, cover up and hold their fists properly. He spent a lot of time teaching them how to punch and deliver a lot of energy by locking their arms and pivoting their bodies into the punch. They would spar around the yard, where Leed could actually out-spar Benji, the better athlete. Leed had a slim body and could out-move and dodge the stouter built body of his younger brother.

On Monday after breakfast Linda talked to Telford, and then he went with her into one of the back rooms and came back with a big box. Before he left for work and the boys left for school, he put the box in the back of the 1941 Ford pickup. Then he went to Red Ledford's farm. Red had given Telford the timber to clear the land so he could expand his pasture. He cut and used the mules to drag logs until late afternoon. These trees were smaller, not real good for logs so when they were in the yard Telford cut them into pulp wood lengths so they could be loaded crossways on the train cars. They would later load them and haul them to the pulp wood yard by the Tallulah Falls Railroad track to be sold for pulp wood.

Telford had told the boys to meet him there after school. When they got there he told them what Linda had told him, "Your mama told me that Mrs. Lewis ain't got no wood for the winter and she felt that the Bible is very clear that we are to care for the widows and fatherless. But Mrs. Lewis' is a real proud woman so she'll try to pay us if we haul her any wood. Your mama sent along that box of scraps so Mrs. Lewis can make them into quilts for us in trade for the wood."

Mrs. Lewis lost her husband Frank, in France, in World War II. She lived in a shack with her mother, Grandma Sherrill, and with her daughter, Cindy, who was a couple of years younger than Leed. Telford and the boys split a good load of wood, stacked it in the truck and set the box of scraps on the top of the wood before heading down on Cutting Bone Creek where the three ladies lived.

Telford backed up to where wood had been stacked before and they started to unload, when Mrs. Lewis came out and asked, "What are you doing, Telford Brown?" He smiled and said, "We had plenty of wood left over on a job up at Red Ledford's farm and we thought you might be able to use some this winter." Mrs. Lewis answered, "Yeah we can use some wood, how much is it a load?"

Telford came back, "We got to get rid of this wood so Red can clear for more pasture so it really ain't fer sale."

"Well I got to pay you something for your time and gas a haulin' it," she returned. Telford then went for the box of scraps and said, "Well, since you are one of the best quilt makers in the whole county, can you make these into quilts for us? Linda's been too busy to get them made, and cold weather is a gettin' here fast."

Mrs. Lewis let out an agreeable smile and said, "Yeah, I can make Linda several quilts out of this many scraps."

"No, she only needs two quilts; one for Leed and one for Benji. You keep the rest and use them yourself."

Leed thought, "Mama puts so many quilts on the bed on cold nights now that we can't even stand our feet straight up because of the weight. Instead we have to lay them over sideways. We shore don't need no more!" But he knew this was his mom's way of going out of her way to help someone.

Cindy had walked out on the porch now and Leed's eyes opened wide as he noticed how much Cindy had grown and how pretty she seemed all of a sudden. His dad had to call twice for Leed to help Benji finish unloading the truck, while he carried the box in the house for Mrs. Lewis.

Mrs. Lewis was a diligent woman and immediately separated out all the larger scraps into a pile that was more than enough to make two quilts. That evening after supper she started looking through the remaining scraps and she had a brilliant idea. Since cold weather was already setting in, and she didn't have the money to buy Cindy a new coat, and the coat she had used for the last two years was way too tight for her, she would use the scraps to make her a new coat. She went over to the pedal sewing machine and got her scissors out, measured Cindy and cut out the inside of the coat from an odd piece of blue cloth she had. She sewed the lining together, then some cotton batting for insulation over that and then started sewing the multi colored scraps in an intricate pattern over the batting to make the coat.

As Mrs. Lewis sewed Grandma Sherrill got out her Bible and told Cindy to sit by her on the floor and listen to her read some verses. She opened her Bible and read in Genesis 37:3 about how Jacob, called Israel by God, loved his son Joseph so much that he gave him a coat of many colors, like her mother was making for her. This made Mrs. Lewis feel good, because times had been real hard after her husband's death and she had not been able to provide some basic needs for her daughter, much less anything special. She worked late into the night; way after Cindy and Grandma Sherrill had gone to bed to finish the 'coat of many colors'.

The next morning Mrs. Lewis handed Cindy the 'coat of many colors' and watched with great satisfaction as she put it on to wear to school. It fit her perfectly and looked really good on her, for a homemade coat.

At the same time the old small school bus that came through the back roads where the Browns and Cindy lived was coming by the Brown farm. To the driver's surprise, there stood Ronnie and Lonnie out on the road waiting on the bus. As he stopped to pick them up he noticed their mom standing behind a tree with a stick to make sure they got on the bus. She was still mad about the car Slewfoot had wrecked, and was forcing the boys to ride the school bus which they hadn't done in a couple of years. As they got on the driver said, "Well I ain't see'd you boys in a long time, why'ya ride'n the bus today fer?" Ronnie, climbing in behind Lonnie, was too sulled up to talk, so he just grunted and shoved Lonnie to the back of the small bus.

Soon they stopped at Mrs. Lewis' shack. As Cindy climbed onto the bus, Ronnie looked at her new coat. As they rode along, Ronnie who was just behind Cindy looked closer at Cindy's 'coat of many colors' and said, "Where'd'ja get that coat girl."

Cindy uncomfortably answered, "My mom made it last night."

Ronnie sneered, "It's made out of scraps."

Cindy now hurt because he was putting down her mom's great

gift said, "This is a 'coat of many colors' like Jacob gave his son Joseph in the Bible."

"That's a joke girl, your mom made that coat, cause ya'll are so poor you can't afford no real coat," Ronnie sneered again.

By the time the bus arrived at school, Cindy was in tears with Ronnie still verbally poking her. Leed and Benji drove up in their mom's car at the same time the bus arrived. They got out and were going to the school house, when Cindy came off the bus squalling, with Ronnie right behind her still making fun of her 'coat of many colors'. Leed, heard Ronnie say something about the coat, then he realized that Cindy was crying. As he looked at her coat it came to him that the coat was made from the scraps that they had taken to Mrs. Lewis the day before. Leed, suddenly realizing what was going on and feeling very protective of the helpless, sobbing girl, dropped his books, stepped between Cindy and Ronnie and shoved Ronnie.

"Leave her alone!" he ordered.

The school principal, who was in the parking lot watching the buses unload, had heard Ronnie aggravating Cindy and was already on the move to stop Ronnie when Leed intervened. He stepped between the two boys before a fight could start and said, "There ain't gonna be no fight'n on school property boys!" Then he thought how much he disliked Ronnie's smart mouth and how he would really like to see Ronnie get straightened out. A quick thought hit him and he followed with, "But I don't have nothing to do with that public road out there, if ya'll want to fight out there, that's beyond my control." He then looked straight into Leed's eyes and gave a slight nod.

Leed understood completely and looking back at Ronnie, said, "If you ain't afraid, why don't ye step out here in the road and take on a man instead of a girl!" Ronnie growled, "I can take you apart!" Leed, now in full rage, snarled "I'm gonna' take you down, Ronnie!"

They both stepped out into the road and started wrestling around. Benji and Lonnie followed them and Benji said, "Leed quit wrestling and start boxing like dad showed ye, get in your stance and get ye guard up!" Leed calmed down, stepped back, crouched, got on the balls of his feet, raised his hands to the boxing position as his dad had taught him, tucked in his elbows to protect his sides and then focused his eyes on the center of Ronnie's upper chest where a person's center of movement is. As he started to dance in front of Ronnie, every thing seemed to be happening in slow motion. He concentrated on each move and was able to hit Ronnie in the nose or mouth at will, and was delivering left hooks to the side of his head with ease.

When Benji gave the advice to Leed, Lonnie looked at him and said, "Now you quit helping him and stay out of this!" Benji grinned at Lonnie and said, "You better shut up fat boy or I'll kick that fat butt of yours."

Lonnie countered with, "I'll body slam ye boy!" and lunged at Benji. Benji easily side-stepped the lunge and gave Lonnie a quick kick in the seat of the pants as he went by. Lonnie turned and lunged again and again, but each time the dancing Benji gave him a good lift of the rear end.

The principal was standing at the edge of the parking lot greatly enjoying himself while Cindy was standing there with her hand over her mouth, wondering if she had started the whole thing. Finally the principal said "That's enough boys." By then blood was pouring out of Ronnie's nose and Benji had Lonnie sprawled out on the road and every time he started to get up, Benji re-deposited him back on the road. Leed and Benji both obeyed the principal and walked over to where he was standing. Ronnie and Lonnie headed up by the gym away from the school.

Then Ronnie stopped and hollered back at Leed, "This ain't over yet Leed!" The brothers stormed out of sight.

The principal smiled, then got stern and looked at everyone standing around and said, "Alright kids I don't want to hear anymore about this! UNDERSTOOD?" He finished with, "Now everyone get to class!"

As the Brown boys headed to the restroom to clean up, Leed noticed out of the corner of his eye that Cindy was looking at him. He strutted to the bathroom wondering, "Could this little girl grow up to be the woman I'm looking for? Aw, she's too young!" was the finish to his thought.

Ronnie and Lonnie caught a ride back home and hid in the barn till the bus came by that afternoon before going into the house.

That evening at home Benji told their dad the entire story of what had happened at school. Telford looked real serious and then turned to Leed and said, "That girl is father-less son, I'm glad that God had you there to take up for her, I'm real proud of you." Then he asked for some details of how the fight went and Benji gave him a blow by blow of the events. That night Linda gave Telford a good talking to about how she didn't like the boys fighting, but she did say she agreed that Leed should have taken up for Cindy. She even thought that Cindy would make a good wife for Leed someday; she didn't tell Telford but kept it in her heart.

CHAPTER

11

HOG KiLLiN'

On Friday Gleyness's sister came and picked her up to spend the night because they were going to Gainesville shopping the next day. With her eyes dancing, she told Ronnie and Lonnie not to drive the pickup while she was gone. She was still mad about them wrecking her car. After she left, Ronnie told Lonnie, "Let's go to town."

"We can't it's too fer to walk!" answered Lonnie. Ronnie said, "We ain't walking I know where the pickup keys are."

"But mama said we couldn't drive the pickup," answered Lonnie.

Ronnie finished with, "I don't care. Let's go."

As they drove on up across the concrete bridge, just below the big trestle that crosses Tiger Creek north of Wiley, Ronnie spoke, "We gotta show people how tough we are Lonnie; let's look for someone to whup!"

Lonnie, with a quick look at Ronnie, answered, "I've had enough of this whuppin' stuff to do me for a while."

"Well let's look around anyway," Ronnie finished.

As Ronnie and Lonnie came on up U.S. 441 through Tiger they got behind an old man driving an old truck and couldn't get around him. Ronnie looked at Lonnie and said, "When we get to the stretch that goes by the Ice Plant and the golf course, on up toward Clayton, I'll pass this guy." When they reached that stretch, however, which was the last place to pass anyone before Clayton, several cars were coming and they couldn't get around the old man. Ronnie was impatient and got right behind him like that would make the trip faster. As they went around the curve by Ramey's Station, then the next curve and started up the hill where L. J. Hunter lived, the old man's head moved across over to the middle of the cab and then turned left and started moving toward the open driver's window. Unknown to Ronnie and Lonnie, his jaws were full of tobacco juice and he needed to get rid of it. Now was that time.

He ejected the tobacco juice out the driver's window, and as it streamed out, it seemed to turn into something alive. This gigantic, swirling, amoeboid, spider like mass came flying through space. Ronnie and Lonnie, both terrified at the approach of this unclean thing, screamed and drew back as it attached itself to the windshield in front of Ronnie's face, in an oozing, drooping mass. As Ronnie drove on they both started gagging and Lonnie covered his eyes, where he wouldn't have to look at it any more and whined, "It got us Ronnie!" but his brother had to keep driving through this gagging ordeal.

They soon came to the Sinclair station in town where they pulled in and got out to look at how bad this monster was attached to the windshield. With revulsion, Ronnie said, "We gotta' wash it off," and grabbed the water hose, which was there at the gas pumps to fill up radiators, and spun the spigot open. When the water came streaming out he directed it at the windshield."

When he did, Lonnie said in a fearful tone, "It's growing!" The tobacco juice was absorbing the water and spreading. It took Ronnie and Lonnie ten minutes and all of the cleaning towels in the holder at the pumps to get the windshield clean.

As they got back in the old truck to leave, Ronnie said, "I hate tobaker juice!"

They drove over the rise on Main Street in Clayton and started down, by Derrick's car garage, where they noticed that one older fellow had parked his car parallel over where there were two slant parking places isolated together Five other guys were leaned up on the car with him, talking, as they watched the cars go by. Ronnie looked at the older guys and said in disgust, "I hate old fellers!" After Ronnie and Lonnie had ridden by several times, Ronnie got an idea and told Lonnie, "Here's what we're a gonna do. I'll slow down and drive by real close to them men right there and you can hold your hand out and slap everyone of them in a row. We'll do a drive by slappin'."

Lonnie objected, "I ain't slappin' nobody, I don't want whupped again!"

Ronnie, now obviously angry said, "Well you drive then and I'll do the slappin'!"

They rode down to the end of town and changed drivers at the turning around place. With Lonnie behind the wheel, the boys drove back through town, and as they passed the old men, Ronnie instructed him on where he was to drive when they came back in the other direction. They turned around at the Sinclair station and headed back. As Lonnie slowed down and got lined up for the run, Ronnie got on his knees on the seat of the pickup, leaned out the window and got his hand ready. Lonnie drove a perfect track and they caught the old men off guard. Ronnie caught the first guy right on the left cheek, as well as the second, the third, the fourth and then came the fifth.

Things were happening so fast that Ronnie didn't remember the cardinal rule of the mountains; 'You don't slap no man on the cheek when he has his jaw's full of tobaker juice', and the fifth guy had a big chew of tobacco in and his jaws was swelled up where he hadn't spit in awhile. Ronnie's hard slap on the fifth fellow's cheek resulted in the immediate ejection of a significant amount of tobacco juice right into Ronnie's face and down his arm. He lost his concentration and missed the sixth fellow completely. Lonnie, not knowing about the fifth fellow, drove on a whooping and a hollering, as Ronnie slid back into the pickup and sat down sputtering and gagging.

When he got where he could talk he ordered Lonnie, "Drive the back streets around them guys before they find us, and take me out to that first turn to the right off of Warwoman Road, to the ford at the little creek out there to clean up." Then Ronnie mumbled, "I hate tobaker juice!" After fifteen minutes in the branch Ronnie finally had himself and the side of the truck cleaned up enough to go home. They took the back roads to the house, so they wouldn't be caught by the fellows from the drive by slapping.

The next day was Saturday and Leed and Benji were waxing their scoot boards because the leaves were in beautiful fall colors and would soon be falling, which should make for the best scoot boarding of the year. As they worked in the shed they witnessed something very amusing. Their dad had to make a trip to town so he came out and got into his 1941 Ford pickup and started to leave. But he'd evidently forgotten something and decided to get out and run back into the house. Since he was parked on level ground, he just knocked the truck out of gear, left the flathead eight engine running, and left the door open.

While he was gone, their mother's favorite pet, her gray tabby cat, ran up, jumped onto the running board then into the floorboard of the pickup and started smelling around. Their dad ran out, jumped into the pickup, put it into gear and took off. About that time the startled cat jumped upon the bench seat by Telford and startled him. He threw the brakes on and slid to a stop. He didn't know that the boys were watching; by now with great delight and interest. Telford at best disliked cats, so he grabbed this cat, even though it was his wife's favorite, and started toward the rolled down window opening on the drivers side to throw it out. But the cat expanded and caught the window opening of the door in four different places. Telford didn't want cat scratches on his truck, so he backed the cat up and tried again. And again the cat expanded and caught the window perimeter. The boys were elated at this sight of their dad and a cat in such a struggle.

Finally Telford grabbed the cat with both hands and tried to poke the cat out the window head first. This didn't work either, because instead of expanding the cat just locked his claws into Telford so tight that he couldn't shake him off. Finally defeated, Telford realized that you can't poke a 14-inch cat through an 18 by 18 window, so he opened the door and carefully dropped the cat down onto the running board and waited to let the cat run off. The boys both gave their dad a rousing, clapping ovation that shocked him since he thought he hadn't been seen. He slammed the door, dumped the clutch, and scattered gravel down the driveway as he got out of there.

When his dad got back, Leed asked him to borrow the pickup to go to Jordan Laycock's to study with him. Telford said, "Sure, son, as long as you and you brother keep quiet about the cat!" Leed smiled and said, "OK."

When he arrived at Mr. Laycock's house, Leed and Mr. Laycock discussed how to work formulae and how to plot a graph and did several problems together, some on the slide rule. Later, when they had finished, Mr. Laycock told Leed, "Son, I think you're ready. I want to give you my old slide rule and I'm going to loan you a book on calculus to help you understand formulae better."

Leed said, "Thanks, Mr. Laycock."

Then Mr. Laycock said, "Now, have you thought about going to Georgia Tech next year, like I asked you awhile back?"

Leed said, "Sure, I would love to go to Georgia Tech and be an engineer like you, but do you think I can make it, or even get into Georgia Tech?"

Mr. Laycock responded, "Son, I know you can make it as smart as you are, and I'll help you get in, but the real question is, can you and your parents afford it?"

Leed hung his head and said, "I'm afraid not. We ain't poor, but my dad and mom don't have that kind of money." Mr. Laycock, his eyes sad with concern said, "Well, son, I'll bring this before the Lord in prayer then."

Leed looked at him and said, "Thank you, Mr. Laycock."

They talked awhile longer and then Leed got ready to go home. As he was heading for the door, Mr. Laycock told him, "Now rabbit season opens in a few weeks and my Beagles are ready to go, so if you don't mind, ask your dad and granddad if I can come out and run them pups."

"You know they don't mind you hunt'in out there, besides that we like to hunt and eat rabbits too," answered Leed.

Mr. Laycock said, "I don't want but one or two rabbits, so y'all hunt with me, so we can get more rabbits and let the dogs run more."

"OK, we'll see you opening day then," answered Leed.

Mr. Laycock told him bye and he drove home thinking about his desire to go to college, but in his mind he knew that it probably wasn't going to happen.

As Telford cut logs during the year he would bring home some of the scrub, or crooked logs and throw them off at his house and at Jeremiah's. He would cut the logs up at Jeremiah's house all along so Jeremiah could work them up at his own pace. But Telford had a big pile of logs out from his barn that needed worked up. He always kept quite a bit of dry wood in the woodshed, but they burned a lot of wood each winter.

He told the boys, "We got to get that wood cut and worked up so it'll have time to dry so we can heat the house this winter. I'll cut and split during the day this week and we'll will split wood and stack it in the wood shed each evening." Telford had wood lying all over the place every evening and they would fly into it and split till dark each night. After supper they would go back out and pile the split wood on the 1941 Ford pickup and haul it over to the wood shed and stack it in the dry.

Friday evening they split wood until dark. When they went in to eat, Telford said, "Boys there's a home football game tonight. Why don't ya'll go and we'll load the wood on the pickup in the morning. We ain't gonna' put it in the shed no how. Your mom has found out that Mrs. Lewis' cousin is taking her and Cindy and Grandma Sherrill to town shopping in the morning. She's picking them up about ten o'clock, so that will give us time to have a load on the truck and be there about ten fifteen. We should have time to unload and come back for at least two more loads before they get back. With the load we've already hauled, that should be enough to get them through the winter. Now ya'll go have a good time."

There was another good crowd at the football game to watch the Wildcats. But it was a lot cooler this time, so they stood around a barrel that had a fire built in it, instead of along the cable. Again Benji was so into the game that he worked as hard around the barrel as most of the players did on the field. Leed managed to stay out of the way of Betty Dewbury. As the night went on, and as he looked at the cheerleaders on the other side of the field, he wondered if any of them would want to know a lonely boy like him. He so wanted a special girl to talk to and share things with. After the game, a worn out Benji and a very lonely and heart-sunken Leed left the crowd behind and went home.

The next morning they pulled off the triple load, undercover, good deed that Linda and her caring heart had conceived. They praised God; it went off without a hitch. About a week later Linda went down to get the two quilts that Mrs. Lewis had made for her. After she had visited inside for a while, the two women walked out on the porch. Mrs. Lewis probed Linda, "Did Telford put all this wood here by my porch?"

Linda answered, "Carol, Telford and them boys is hauling wood all the time, in every direction, they ain't no tellin' where you might find wood scattered to." Mrs. Lewis smiled, held back a tear and hugged Linda, and said, "Thank you Linda, I hope these quilts are a blessing to you and your family like ya'll are to us."

It was getting on close to Thanksgiving and the weather had turned off good and cold. It had frosted Thursday morning and again Friday morning, so on Friday evening Telford told the boys that it was fit weather to kill the hogs the next morning. He said, "I've already got the tables outside in front of the kitchen, I've got the barrel clean and partly full of water to dip the hogs in, with a pile of wood laid around it. And I cleaned the pot to render out the lard in, so we'll hit it early tomorrow."

The next morning Telford was up before daylight. He went out and lit the fire under the barrel to get the water hot enough to release the hair off the hogs so they could scrape them. By the time the boys got up, he was back in the house sipping coffee. Leed liked this time of year and especially hog killing time. It was hard work, but provided a lot of food to help the family get through the winter, when logging was hard and very limited by the weather. Money could get real tight if it was a bad winter and the trips to the grocery store had to be stretched. Plus, Leed thought, that working up meat was real interesting because it involved so many processes.

After a quick snack to tide the boys over they went out and

backed the pickup up to the hog pen. They had two hogs in the fatting pen ready to kill now. Telford shot one hog between the eyes, then the other, to dispatch them instantly. The boys immediately tore out the end of the hog pen and, with their dad's help, they dragged both hogs up into the back of the pickup. They drove over and backed up to the barrel of hot water so they could dip the hogs. There was a big limb up over the barrel where Telford had attached a block and tackle to so they could hoist the hogs. They had a single-tree hooked to the hoist so they lowered it down and hooked the hook on each end of the single-tree in a slit cut behind the main leader, in the back legs of the hogs. Telford dipped his finger in the water in the barrel and checked the temperature. When it was to his liking, the first hog was hoisted up and lowered into the barrel of hot but not boiling water. Boiling water would set the hair on the hog, making it difficult to scrape off.

After a short time in the barrel, the first hog was hoisted out and laid back in the truck. When the second hog was hoisted up and over the barrel, Telford dipped it while the boys went to scraping the hair off of the first animal. They had big, sharp butcher knifes that they held with both hands. While holding the blade crossways, they drew them across the hog like a straight razor to scrape the hair off. Like shaving. The boys made quick work of the first hog and then the second.

When they finished they took a stick and moved the rope farther out on the limb that was holding the block and tackle, and then pulled the pickup up a little, so they would have room to gut the hogs. They hoisted the first hog up and threw a couple of buckets of water on him and then Telford handed Benji several buckets of water up in the back of the truck and he washed the other hog and the back of the truck clean. As Telford gutted the hogs the boys cut out the livers and took them to their mom who would make liver mush out of them later. When they picked up the other hog, they finished washing it and the bed of the truck where it had been laying, because Telford made sure everything was kept clean.

As each hog was still hanging, after being gutted, and the head removed, they took a hand saw and split him right down the middle of the spine, then loaded the halves in the pickup bed. While this was going on, Jeremiah drove up. When the heads and feet were cut off the hogs they were laid with the hog halves in the back of the pickup waiting on Jeremiah, who took the parts and laid them on a sack in the back of his truck. He and Ruby were going to make souse meat out of the heads and he would pickle the feet. After he left, Telford told the boys, "We don't make souse meat because dad and mom made it all the time when I was a boy and I never did like it, so we just give it to them."

Benji said, "Good I don't like it much either when we have to eat it down at Grandma's."

When they had processed the hogs into halves, they drove them up to the house then backed the truck up to the tables, where they would work up one half at a time. The tables were each assigned so that a certain process would take place on each.

Linda had a hot fire going in the stove, coffee perking in the pot, a greased skillet heating and a big pan of biscuits already in the oven. Then, as the first item of business, Telford stripped the tenderloin out of the first hog half and walked up the steps and handed it to his wife who sliced, floured and dropped the slices in the hot grease in the skillet. Soon she took up the tenderloin, started scrambling eggs in another greased skillet and made gravy in the skillet where she had just fried the tenderloin.

When everything was ready, she called the hungry crew in to an awesome breakfast. This was the main reason that Leed liked hog killing time so much; fresh tenderloin fried golden brown with scrambled eggs and biscuits broken open with gravy over the top. It didn't get no better than that. When they were finished with the main part of the meal, they took a couple of biscuits, which they had loaded with butter when the meal started so it would melt good, and put big spoons-full of blackberry jelly on them. Boy was it good. They washed it all down with good, cold sweet milk.

After breakfast they went back to work. Telford would take a hog half and skillfully cut the shoulder, ham and middlin' out. Benji's job was to cut all four shoulders into one inch pieces for grinding into sausage. He had one washtub just for that. Leed was cutting up into chunks all the excess fat that Telford cut off, and throwing them into another wash tub. Later they would mix a certain proportion of fat with the shoulder meat to grind as sausage, while the rest would be rendered out to make lard and cracklings. As Telford cut each half up, he would take the hams and middlins' up to the meat house, which was the curing room on the end of the porch.

When Telford had cut up the last half, he left the boys cutting and went up to the meat house and started applying the seasoning to the hams and middlins' so they would cure out. He rubbed the big hams with salt and then brown sugar mixed with some spices and laid them out on a shelf to cure. Later he would place them in sacks and hang them up. Then he rubbed the middlins' the same way. The middlins' would be left lying flat on the shelf where they could easily be sliced later. The part of the middlins' where there were no streaks of lean meat would be cut into fatback for seasoning or frying. The part where there were streaks of lean meat would be cut into streak of lean, also called bacon.

When the meat was all cut up, Telford and Benji clamped the meat grinder on the edge of one table and started grinding the sausage. Telford made sure the percentage of fat and lean was correct and that the proper amount of sage, black and red pepper were added. Stout-armed Benji got to turn the handle of the grinder.

Leed went to where the big black cast iron pot was sitting up on rocks to hold it at the right height for laying a fire under it. He laid kindling and wood under the pot and lit the kindling up to start a fire for heating the pot, so he could render the lard out of the pieces of fat he had cut up. He went back up and got Benji to stop for a minute to help him carry the washtub full of fat pieces down to the pot. He then loaded the pot about one third full and used a stick to stir the fat pieces so they wouldn't stick to the iron pot, while he cooked the lard out of them. As a pool of grease was formed, he added more fat pieces. Leed then went quickly to the house where he got the metal lard buckets and brought them back to the rendering pot.

After a while he had a good pool of lard to work with, so he was able to cook faster, now that the heat no longer caused the fat pieces to stick to the side of the pot before they became cracklings. He stoked up the fire to accelerate the rendering process. When he had the pot about two thirds full, he stopped adding pieces of fat so they all cooked down into cracklings. He then dipped out the cracklings with a screened dipper he had and put them in the small lard bucket. Next he dipped the lard over into the big lard bucket with a long handle boiler, leaving a pool of lard in the pot to work with. Then he added more fat pieces to the pool of lard and cooked them down. He continued this process until the pot was two thirds full of lard again, when he again dipped the cracklings and lard out into the buckets.

This process took Leed until dark, so he put on a coat, kept the fire going and worked right on. He added wood around the pot regularly to keep the rendering process going. Whenever he added wood to the fire, Leed would take the stirring stick out of the lard and drip hot liquid grease onto the remaining coals. This quickly ignited and accelerated the fire to keep the pot hot. When he was finally finished, he let the fire die down, dipped the remaining lard into the bucket and laid the lids on the containers to allow them to cool until the next day. They were too hot to handle.

While Leed had spent the day and evening rendering out lard, Telford, Linda and Benji were also busy, cutting everything up, salting the hams and middlins' and grinding sausage. They carried the tub of sausage in the house and cleaned up outside. Afterward they went back to the kitchen and packed the sausage into the jars that Linda had scalded. Then Linda placed new lids and rings on the filled quart jars and placed them into the canner. She poured boiling water around the jars and placed the canner on the wood cook stove to heat up. When the gage showed fifteen pounds of pressure she held it there for fifty minutes to kill all the bacteria in the meat, so the sausage would keep. This process went well into the night, consuming much firewood and keeping the kitchen hot. The last jars were pulled out of the canner the next morning.

12 LEAVES

R abbit season opened the Saturday before Thanksgiving, and Mr. Laycock came by earlier that week, talked to Telford and set a time to meet on Saturday morning to hunt. Saturday morning Telford got Leed and Benji up early; they ate breakfast and were out at the barn to meet Mr. Laycock by 7:30. The engineer backed up his 1953 GMC Hydramatic, got out and let the tailgate down. Telford and the boys shook hands with their guest and each looked at the others guns. Mr. Laycock had a 12-gauge, A5 Browning semiautomatic shotgun, Telford had his 12-gauge Stevens double barrel shotgun. Leed was hunting with his dad's 12- gauge Stevens single barrel shotgun, while Benji was stuck with his dad's 20-gauge Stevens single barrel.

They all bowed down on one knee, while Telford prayed for their safety and for a successful hunt. After the prayer, Leed and Benji checked out the dog box in the back of Mr. Laycock's pickup, a rare sight in the mountains. As Mr. Laycock got each Beagle out of the nice dog box, he made introduction, "This is Danny Boy, my old standby, and this is his sister, Daisy. They're registered red and whites." This denoted their color combination. He continued, "Now this is Dakota and Sassy; they're registered red and whites, too. I brought them in from another blood-line to introduce new stock. I hope they'll produce some fine dogs by breeding Danny Boy to Sassy and Dakota to Daisy."

After turning the dogs out, they did all the stuff that dogs do before they're ready to hunt, and then took off with their tails a-wagging. Soon Danny Boy was working hard along a fence row in some bushes, when he jumped a rabbit. He let out a squall and the other dogs fell in behind him. The race was on. Their voices made fine music as they chased the rabbit down toward Jeremiah and Ruby's place, then circled around and came back up the fence row. When the rabbit came through an opening, Telford fired and rolled the first rabbit. He went over and picked up the animal and let the dogs get a good smell of it, then told them to get back at it. They scattered out and soon had another rabbit on the run. This one made the mistake of heading straight toward Mr. Laycock who dispatched him straight away. By late morning they had enough rabbits for everybody, so Mr. Laycock loaded the dogs up, thanked Telford and told everyone goodbye.

That afternoon Leed and Benji took the scoot boards out for a test on the thick bed of leaves that had fallen in the woods over the last few weeks. This time, they climbed up to where Crumley Mountain got pretty steep and started scooting. They found out two things: the thick bed of leaves made the scoot boards a lot faster and, they offered much more control. Soon Leed was doing some pretty good stuff on his scoot board. But Benji was flying, doing quick turns, jumps and even jumped up in the air and turned his board sideways and slid down a small, slick dead tree lying on the ground, then jumped up and landed back on the leaves and scooted on. They had a great time on the mountain before scoot boarding all the way back to the edge of their property and walking home.

Mr. Laycock had Leed coming over to work and study with him about once a week and he was amazed at how smart the young man was and how fast he grasped new, even very technical ideas. One day the following week, Mr. Laycock met Telford in town and told him how well Leed was doing in his extra studies.

Telford said, "Yeah, he is as smart as his grandpa; I guess it jumped my generation."

Mr. Laycock said, "I think he would do very well down at Georgia Tech and I know he would make a great engineer with all of the practical things that you've already taught him as his basis. Telford, do you think you can afford to send him to college?"

Telford thought for a minute before he answered, "Well Jordan, I don't have that kind of money and you know it. I would sell part of the farm if that's what it took to send that boy to college, but I can't. When dad gave me all that land he just asked one thing: that I wouldn't sell it, but pass it on to my kids. So I just don't see no way, but I will talk with his mom about it."

Mr. Laycock put his hand on Telford's shoulder and said, "I tell you what Telford, let's covenant together to bring this before God in prayer every day so we can see Him do something great!"

"Thank you, Jordan. I agree, that's the thing to do," answered Telford.

Thanksgiving at the Brown's was held at Grandpa and Grandma's house. Ruby made sure of that. It was awesome, too, with a mother and grandmother that were such good cooks. Glenysis and the twins would not be there, because Latimer never allowed them or himself to associate with anybody. Leed's mom and Ruby had been cooking pies and cakes for two days, and spent all Thursday morning cooking two big hens, a ham, a boiler of leather britches, a pot of mashed taters, a pan of dressing, a big pan of sweet taters with butter and brown sugar all over them, cornbread and biscuits. Early afternoon brought everyone together around the two tables they had set up in Jeremiah and Ruby's living room. Then Telford asked everyone to bow their heads and he prayed, "Father thank You for blessing us so well this year, for taking care of us, for bringing the war in Korea to an end and for protecting our sons Larry and Ronald while they served their country over there. Now we ask that you would bless this food to nourish our bodies for your service. We ask these things in the name of our Lord, Jesus Christ." Everyone dove in and enjoyed the feast spread before them.

The next week Telford informed the boys, "The field corn is dry and we better take a few days off and pick it. When ya'll get home from school we'll start gathering corn." After school they took the pickup and drove along getting six rows at a time. Telford drove down two rows knocking the corn down. Benji walked behind the pickup and pulled the corn off those stalks and threw it in the back of the pickup, while Telford picked the two rows on the driver's side of the pickup and Leed got the two rows on the passenger side. They would fill the bed of the pickup up pretty quick this way, and then take it to the barn and throw it into the corn bins.

By Friday they got down in the bottom land, into the good corn with big ears. After they got the truck loaded, Telford told the boys, "When we get to the barn I want you boys to shell part of this load and we'll take it to the mill to grind into cornmeal tomorrow. Your mom says we're getting low. We'll take the rest of the load to grind into feed for the stock, so don't unload the truck except for the corn you shell."

The boys took the load to the barn. After shucking a big pile of corn, they set a big number three washtub under the corn sheller. Benji turned the handle on the sheller while Leed dropped the corn down into the chute. As Leed fed in whole ears of corn at the top, the grains of corn poured out the bottom while the cobs were ejected out the side and went into a box. The cobs would later be dumped into the box in the kitchen to be used as kindling to start fires in the wood cook-stove. With Benji providing the muscle for turning the handle, and Leed dropping corn in with both hands, the job didn't take long and they had the number three wash tub nearly full. They loaded it in with the corn in the back of the pickup and were ready to go to the mill.

They got up the next morning, which was Saturday, and after breakfast the boys got in the pickup with their dad and headed up to Tiger and went up Bridge Creek Road to Crunkleton's Mill. When they got there, Telford backed the pickup up to the chute for the whole corn and the boys toted the wash tub full of shelled corn inside. Dave Crunkleton the owner, fired up his caterpillar power plant, engaged the clutch, and started the big flat belt to slapping as it drove the pulleys to the big grinder. Then Leed and Benji went out to the pickup and started pushing corn down the chute first with their feet and then with a big shovel that Dave kept by the door. Telford was inside putting big sacks under the bottom of the hopper and filling them up, one after another while the coarse corn feed was grinding. When they finished grinding the feed corn, Dave disengaged the clutch to the big grinder and engaged the one to the small grinder. Benji poured the corn in the hopper with a big scoop while Leed volunteered to sack up the cornmeal with the 10 lb. sacks on the other end. He always loved this part of going to the mill; he enjoyed catching the fresh meal coming out of the grinder in his hand, how soft and warm it felt as it went into the sacks. When they were through, Dave took a portion of the meal and feed as payment and the Browns headed home.

Back at the house they put the ten pound sacks of corn meal in the kitchen, the sacks of feed in the barn, went to the shed and got their scoot boards and headed to Crumley Mountain. After they had been scooting for a while, they looked down the hollow and saw someone coming. Benji recognized who it was first and hollered, "Come on Tommy Hawk, the scootin's good." Tommy Hawk had come to the house looking for Leed and Benji, and their parents had told him where they were, and so he grabbed the other scoot board and came on up the mountain. The boys were getting very good at scoot boarding and were racing and cutting each other off and doing all kind of crazy things. Benji even ran up on the leaves on a pile of dirt that made a ramp and did a back flip off the ramp and almost landed it. Finally, a worn out crew scooted down the mountain and walked on home in time for supper.

The boys only had a couple more weeks of school left before they got off for more than a week for Christmas. When they went back to school that Monday everyone was getting ready for tests and Leed and Benji were studying hard at night after supper until bedtime. One night Leed had been helping Benji, who didn't have quite the take for book learning that Leed had. The older brother was helping his younger brother learn about energy and heat transfer for science class. After they put up their books, they went into their cold bedroom. It was really frigid outside that night and their house only had a heater in the front room.

Benji said, "It's cold in here I wish that heat in the front room would transfer in here."

Leed said, "The best way to make that happen is to blow the air into the bedroom like modern central heat systems do."

"But if you blow air in here wouldn't it get cold like the wind blow'n outside?" asked Benji.

114

"No," Leed grinned, "you have a heat source that heats the air, a fan that blows the air, duct work to take the air to the room and more duct to bring it back to the heat source to heat it again. It just goes in circles and keeps each room in a house warm."

"Wow! What will they thank of next!" pondered Benji as they slid into their beds and started the normal routine they always performed, on a real cold night like tonight. First they slid in between the cold sheets and curled up in a ball under all the layers of cover that mom had put on each of their beds. Then, after they had warmed a small area around them, they started sliding their feet down a little at a time, warming it up as they went and finally by the time they had warmed up enough bed to lay out flat, they were asleep.

Christmas was on a Friday and school was out all week. Telford didn't have any logs to load so on Tuesday he took Leed to town with him to take care of some business at the courthouse. After that task was accomplished, Telford asked Leed "How'da'ja like to meet Bob Vickers, the Judge of the Ordinary, the guy that runs Rabun County?"

Leed said, "Yeah I'd like that." They walked in and Telford introduced Leed to Bob and they shook hands. About that time the phone rang and Bob laid down his cigar, picked up the receiver and answered it. Bob was a stout built man who talked loud, so Telford and Leed heard his side of the conversation quite well. Bob said, "Hello." He listened to the phone for several seconds and then said, "What'da'ya mean you forgot your shovels, Jeb?" Telford and Leed both knew he was talking to Jeb Nix, a fellow who ran one of the road crews for the county. Bob listened to Jeb's response and then answered, "No, you're all the way down at the end of Warwoman Road at Pine Mountain, don't drive up here to get your shovels. You'll waste the whole day that way! I'll send Terry down with your shovels." Bob listened intently again and then exploded, "What do you mean, what do I want you to do till he gets there? I tell you what to do, why don't you just lean on each other till Terry gets there, with your shovels and then you can lean on them!"

Then he slammed the phone down, grabbed his short stogie and stormed out of the office.

Telford and Leed walked out of the office grinning. In the foyer they met a slim man in a new pair of overalls coming in the courthouse door. The guy said, "Hello, Telford, and stuck out his hand."

Telford said, "Hello," and shook his hand then introduced Leed and the man, "This is my son Leed. Leed this is Harold Cannon."

Harold stuck his hand out and shook hands with Leed and said, "Hello young man, how old are you?"

"Seventeen sir."

"Well when is your birthday?" Leed respectfully returned, "February fifth."

Harold came right back with, "Good, I'm going to run for state representative next fall and you'll be old enough to vote for me. I want to go to Atlanter and straighten out them high spenders in the legislature down there. Will you vote for me, Leed?"

Leed grinned, because he liked this man's drive, so he said, "Yes I will." Harold and Telford talked a while longer and then Leed followed his dad out to the truck where they got in and headed up towards Main Street.

Telford asked Leed, "How about a hamburger for lunch son." "Sure," came Leed's swift answer. Hamburgers were a rare treat for a boy raised in the mountains. They drove up and turned left on Main Street and pulled into an empty parking spot just below the Standard station. Telford got out and put some money in the parking meter. As Leed stood by the truck a big man in overalls walked up to Telford and grinned. Telford said, "Well, hello L. J., how are you." The man nodded and said, "Good." Telford then motioned for Leed to come up on the sidewalk. When he did Telford introduced them, "L. J. this is my son Leed and Leed this is L. J. Hunter."

By the look on the man's face Leed could tell he was different but he smiled at Leed and with a gruff, slow and peaceable voice he said, "Good to meet you Leed." Leed answered, "It's good to meet you L. J. how have you been doing?"

He nodded and returned a, "Good to tolerable."

116

Then Telford asked, "L. J. how old are you now?"

L. J. leaned forward, rubbed the thick stubble on his chin as he thought and said, "Well I don't know Telford, but I was born when maters gets ripe." Telford grinned and said, "Well you were born in July then, that's good."

Leed thought, "Well this feller's pretty sharp because everybody in the mountains looked forward to the time when tomatoes get ripe. It was like a holiday when you could go to the garden and get a beautiful, red, ripe tomato and bring it into the house to eat. Leed smiled as he realized that L. J. recognized it as almost another season." They talked a few more minutes and then told L. J. goodbye.

They walked across the street to Kermit Brown's hamburger place and went in. Leed's nose turned a flip at the wonderful smell of hamburgers as they walked in and sat down on the stools along the bar. Leed felt like a man sitting there tall with his dad.

Kermit took their order and pinned the order ticket over a big flat frying area where an old man was laboring over cooking hamburgers. One fellow sitting at the other end of the bar, who obviously had a few drinks before he came in, was giving the old man a hard time about how slow he was cooking the hamburgers. Telford and Leed listened in on their conversation.

The drunk said, "Earl you're the slowest cook I've ever seed before." The cook tried to ignore him but he came right back and told the cook, "In fact, I can eat them hamburgers just as fast as you can fix 'em!"

The cook now came back at him without even looking, "Yeah, but fer how long?"

The drunken fellow leaned forward and stated, "Till I starve to death!" The whole place erupted in laughter; the cook just shook his head and kept at his job. Soon Kermit sat a fine big hamburger and a coke in the bottle in front of Telford and Leed and they too-quickly devoured the feast in front of them. Telford paid and they went out to the truck and headed home as Leed thought how much he liked being with his dad.

Down the road a piece, they saw Loge Rogers coming up the road, walking like always. Leed, in a real good mood, waved real big in plenty of time and Loge, now wearing a railroad jacket, returned his characteristic quick up and down wave as the jacket flopped on his arm.

Christmas was a very special time at the Brown home and Telford made sure that none of his family would forget what the celebration was all about. On Christmas morning, since the boys were about grown now, Telford told Linda to fix breakfast and then they would open the few presents they had. After they finished breakfast he read the Christmas story out of Matthew 1:18 through the end of Chapter 2. Then they opened the presents; Linda first, then the boys, and last Telford. Telford made sure that Linda got something she had wanted, the last LP record by Hank Williams that came out after his death earlier that year. The boys each got a new pair of boots, which were a good investment for their dad to get his two loggers. And Linda had a nice new shirt for Telford to wear to church.

They took it easy the rest of the day until they got ready and went to church that evening, where they had a candlelight Lord's Supper to celebrate the birthday of Jesus. Leed always felt uneasy at the Lord's Supper because Preacher Bill always made it clear that the Lord's Supper was a memorial to look back at what Jesus as the Christ had done on the cross, and to look forward to His soon return. He also emphasized that it was only for those who had placed their trust in Jesus Christ as their personal Savior and Lord. So when the unleavened bread, then the little cups of juice came by, he just looked down and passed them on. The thought of Jesus making a soon return for His own got Leed to thinking more about his eternal state. This thought would dominate his thinking for the next few weeks as the dark days of winter were setting in.

13

SNOW

L eed was gripped by doubts of his eternal destiny. To keep his mind off these deep thoughts, and to help the dark winter days to pass, Leed dug into his books at school and the engineering books at home. Sometimes he wondered why he was even working so hard on the engineering books. He knew his chances of going to Georgia Tech were slim. Or none.

One Friday night it was already dark and Leed had to go to the outhouse. He didn't like using the honey pot in the house, unless it was just number one, and even then only in the middle of the night. The moon lit up the trail to the outhouse fine, but it was cold and the wind was blowing hard out of the northwest and hitting high up on Crumley Mountain. That steady cold, roaring sound chilled Leed before he even got cold. He thought, "You gotta go bad to come out to the outhouse on a night like this." By the time he was through and had run all the way back to the house, he was sure enough chilled. He ran into the front room, slammed the door, went to the heater, opened it up, dropped in two more sticks of wood and then almost hugged the heater to get warm.

The next morning he got up earlier than normal, picked up one of the engineering books and followed his mom into the kitchen. He sat down at the table and opened his book up while his mom went swiftly about her job of making breakfast. As she started he thought about how he had seen her do this hundreds of times, but never had paid that much attention. This time he did. First she took the lifter and picked up the two eyes and the crosspiece over the firebox of the wood cook stove and laid them one at a time over

120

in the middle of the stove out of the way. Next she grabbed a handful of white pine cones from a bucket by the stove, then a couple of slivers of rich pine lighter from another bucket and laid the white pine cones down on the grates in the firebox, then the pine lighter on top of the pine cones. Now she placed some cobs and small pieces of kindling, from the same bucket that held the lighter, then filled the fire box up with the stove wood from another bucket and a big box by the door.

She quickly laid the crosspiece and the two eyes back over the now loaded firebox and reached over in the middle of the stove, at the back and slid the damper open to allow the draft to start when she lit the fire. Next she reached up above the wood buckets and pulled a match out of the big match box holder on the wall. She opened the two doors to access the front of the fire box and lit one of the pine cones, closed the doors and reached on the side of the stove and slid the air inlet wide open.

Next she walked over to the Hoosier cabinet and pulled a bowl down from the top and placed her sifter into the bowl and positioned it under the built-in hopper on the left side that she kept full of flour. She pulled the cap off the bottom of the hopper and turned the handle until she had the amount of flour she wanted in the sifter. She then took a box of Arm and Hammer Baking Soda and shook some in the sifter without even measuring. Leed thought, "She really is a great cook because her biscuits are always good."

She turned quickly and Leed had to shift his gaze back to the book to keep her from seeing the keen interest he had in her morning. She went straight to the stove and slid the damper closed so the oven would start heating. Leed had studied the function of this wood cook stove long ago, and it was pretty complicated.

The oven was a cast iron box encased inside the cast iron cook stove. The firebox heated the left side of the oven directly then the hot gases left the firebox and headed across the top of the oven under the eyes so you could cook with a frying pan or boiler. From there, a metal divider forced all the hot gases down the right side and back under the oven, but only on the front half. At the bottom left, over near the firebox, the dividing wall ended. The hot gases now traveled around the end of this separator and then back along the divider, under the back of the oven box, up the back part of the right side of the oven box and now on top for a short ways where they exited up the stove pipe, then out the flue.

But the problem was, the hot air wanted to rise so it would not go down around the oven box on its own and then back up, so that's why his mom opened the damper until the fire got to going good. This created enough draft up the stove pipe and chimney, so when she closed the damper later, this draft pulled the hot gases down and around the oven box so it would get hot enough to cook biscuits. As the hot gases passed down and back up the end, they also heated water in a tank on the right side of the cook stove. His mom would use this hot water to wash dishes after cooking.

Now she shook the sifter up and down a couple of times to mix a little. Then she sifted the flour and baking soda into the bowl, grabbed a big spoon, reached down by the stove, raised the lid on the lard bucket, got a spoon full of lard, pushed the lid back down and shook the lard off the spoon into the bowl. Next she mashed the lard into the flour with a wooden handled wire device. After that, she poured some buttermilk into the bowl and mixed it till she got it just right.

Now she sifted a little more flour out in her hand and spread it over the Hoosier metal table and dumped out the flour ball on the loose flour, sprinkled some more loose flour on top of it and rolled it out flat with a rolling pin she had coated with flour. She cut biscuits out of the flat flour with a Mason jar lid band, and put them on a baking pan and slid them in the oven, after noting the temperature on the gauge was on four hundred and fifty degrees.

She quickly loaded the small fire box back full with stove wood, pulled a frying pan down from the top of the warmer, laid it on the stove, opened a quart jar of sausage and spooned out a bunch into the frying pan. When the sausage was about done, she flopped another frying pan down on the stove, cracked a bunch of eggs in it, took the sausage up in a bowl, dumped in some flour in the grease where the sausage was, stirred it a little then poured in about a quart of milk.

Next she quickly shook salt and pepper on the eggs and gravy, turned to Leed, who was amazed at her speed and concentration, and said, "You stir the gravy while I finish the eggs. In a minute she slid the eggs over to the water tank lid where it wasn't very hot and went to get Telford and Benji for breakfast.

As he stirred hard, scraping the bottom of the cast iron frying pan to keep the gravy from sticking as it thickened, Leed just smiled, shook his head, and thought, "Wow I'm tired and I just watched. What a mom!" They enjoyed a great breakfast that took a lot of work by an awesome mom and wife, but not a lot of time.

Over the next couple of weeks Leed really immersed himself in the hard problems that he found in the engineering books so that he could really understand the concepts that they were trying to teach him. He enjoyed that, knowing that the writers of the textbook had done their job well on some hard subjects.

On the twenty-first day of January, on a Thursday morning, Leed and Benji were awakened by their mom saying these wonderful words, "It snowed boys." They jumped up and looked out the window to find deep snow. And it was still snowing. This meant that there wouldn't be any school that day or on the morrow, so they looked at each other and said, "Scoot boarding." After breakfast Telford looked at the boys and said, "I need to go to town y'all want to come along?" They both said, "Yes," and then Linda frowned, looking at Telford, and asked, "What do you need in town?"

Telford stammered, "Well, ah, ah... we need some bread." She knew then that they just wanted adventure so she said, "Well, ya'll be careful then."

They dressed in the warmest clothes they had and put on their biggest coats and gloves. As they walked out the door, Leed asked his dad, "Do you think the pickup will make it to town dad?"

"No, you couldn't even turn it around here in the yard in ten inches of snow!"

Benji probed, "Well are we gonna' walk?" "No," answered Telford, "we're gonna' borrow your grandpa's old Model-T, it'll go anywhere." Leed then thought of the old Model-T in Jeremiah's barn and how grandpa had tied all of the big ropes around the rear spoke wheels so he could climb up the old road that goes to the top of Crumley Mountain.

After asking grandpa for the Model-T they went to the barn

where Telford raised one side of the hood and poured some gas in the little breather cover and then closed the hood and got in. Benji spun the crank until it started with a sputter. They jumped in and took off towards town. The narrow wheels cut into the deep snow and stirred well while the roped rear wheels dug in and pushed them right on up the road. As they puttered nearer to town, they came around a curve to find the road blocked by a pine tree that had fallen across a power line and was hanging out over the road.

Leed said, "Look at the funny goose-neck looking thang up there; let's go see what it is." As they walked up they saw Jordan Laycock and several Georgia Power linemen looking up at the strange new device that Leed could now see was mounted on the back of a brand new, dual wheel 1954 Chevrolet truck.

Jordan turned and said hello to Telford and the boys.

Telford asked, "What's that mounted on that truck there, Jordan?"

"Well that's our new 'Tree Lift' Telford. We use it to cut tree limbs, work on lines and poles or anything else up off the ground," was Jordan's answer.

About that time Jordan asked them to step back, and as they did, two linemen climbed up on the truck and each of them got into one of the two tubs that were attached on each side of the end of the goose-neck device. One of the tubs had a bunch of control levers on the side of it, with hoses running back down the goose-neck part. The lineman in that tub pulled a lever, the motor of the truck revved up and the tubs picked him and the other lineman up at the same time. He was able to move the neck and the tubs all around. The lineman in the other tub then took a saw and cut limbs, while the lineman with the levers helped push them away from him so they would fall to the ground safely.

They moved, sawed more limbs and kept at it until they had cut the tree right off of the power line. At the same time, the other linemen on the ground were throwing the limbs out of the way and soon the road was clear. Telford and the boys kept talking about the amazing 'Tree Lift' on the way into town and on the way back home.

They stopped on the way back home and picked up Tommy Hawk and he brought extra clothes to spend the night so they could scoot board for a couple of days. Back home they waxed the boards real good and went to the upper end of the pasture, where it was pretty steep and started scooting. With all of the snow on the ground the fear of falling was gone and they all started acting like Benji.

After a while they found an old rotten apple tree trunk that had fallen down on the upper terrace. They dragged it over and laid it along the edge of the terrace and piled and packed snow behind it until they had a huge ramp. Then they would go all the way up into the woods and come down across the upper field at full speed and make high jumps. Each time they got braver and started cutting flips and turning around in the air knowing the thick snow would cushion their fall. Leed could land one every now and then, but Benji and Tommy Hawk were getting real good at jumping and landing. They scoot boarded until they were so cold and hungry that they finally scooted all the way to the house.

They came in, took their boots off and all got around the heater in the front room and started warming their feet. They would hold their cold, red, wet hands up close to the heater until they started hurting then they would put them back against their clothes. Their mom came in and asked, "Anybody hungry?" Every one of them said, "Yes." She said, "Ya'll stay in here and warm up, I'll call when it's ready." They heard the distant sounds of their mom building a fire in the cook stove and of pots and fry pans clanging and after about forty-five minutes, she came and got some very hungry boys who were just about warmed up.

When they walked into the kitchen Benji let out a whoop and said, "Thanks mom that's my favorite, chocolate gravy and biscuits!" The boys sat down and after the prayer they each took a biscuit and broke it open and laid it on the plate. Then they spread fresh butter on each side and put the hot chocolate gravy over the top of the butter biscuit. They never slowed down until all of the biscuits and gravy were gone and Benji had licked the big spoon clean.

The next morning after breakfast the boys re-waxed their boards and headed back up the mountain. As they walked, Leed noticed that the snow had melted a little the day before on top, and it had refrozen into a hard crust during the cold night. He told Benji and Tommy Hawk that they had better not jump because the landing wouldn't be soft enough. They didn't jump, but they found that the crust made the scoot boards very, very fast, so they made many long sweeping runs down through the upper fields all the way to the bottom. This was fun but they tired after a few hours from the long climb back up through all of the fields. They were home by lunch and ate their fill of soup beans and cornbread and teamed up to drink a gallon of sweet milk. Then they went into the front room, lay down and dozed off.

After they awoke Benji started telling Tommy about the night that he and Leed went up to the still and got shot at. Even though he was talking low his mom, with ears like a doe deer, heard some of what he said as she entered the hallway coming from the kitchen. She immediately came in and made Benji repeat his story. Then she called his dad in and made him repeat it again. Linda, completely beside herself, asked Tommy Hawk to go home and then fussed the boys out and asked them, "How could you have done something that stupid?" She then sent them to bed. Telford looked as the boys went by on the way to their room and said, "Boys, I just praise the Lord y'all weren't hurt, or killed," and he placed his hand on Leed shoulder and squeezed it hard.

The next morning they all sat around the breakfast table as Linda slammed the food on the table. After she set everything on the table, she finally exploded, "I still don't see how you boys could have done anything that stupid. I ain't got no food for either of you!" and she went and got both Leed and Benji's plate's and put them on the Hoosier. The boys started to get up but Linda said, "Set down, you ain't going nowhere!"

When she sat down they all bowed their heads and Telford sat for a long time before he finally got out a sobbing, "Thank you Lord for protecting my boys, Amen." When he finished, Linda dumped eggs, gravy, sausage and biscuits into Telford's plate and then dumped some in her plate. Telford continued looking down for a long while before he finally slid his plate over between the boys and said, "I've got food and I give it to you two." He then hung his head back down.

As the silence protracted, Leed realized that his father was sacrificing his breakfast for them. As this sunk in, he knew that he didn't deserve it. Finally, overwhelmed, he got up crying and went into the bedroom where he dropped to his knees and leaned over his bed sobbing.

Nobody talked much the rest of the weekend and Leed just kept his head down at Sunday School, during the morning service and also at the Sunday night service.

The next Monday Ronnie and Lonnie were finally allowed to drive their dad's old work pickup to school. When they got out at school and started walking across the parking lot, Lonnie started skipping and singing, "How much is that doggie in the winder, arf, arf, the one with the waggely tail?" Then Ronnie turned and looked at him with disbelief and slapped him as he was going by. "Where'd'ja learn that?"

Lonnie said, "Don't hit me, I don't like bein' hit."

"Well where'd you learn it at then?" demanded Ronnie.

"From mama's radio station," Lonnie said with pooched out lips. "Well don't sang it out cheer in front of nobody, its embrassin'! You got it?" scowled Ronnie.

CHAPTER 14

TALLULAH GORGE

After school Leed and Benji were on their way home, when they saw Jordan Laycock stopped with a Georgia Power crew on the road. They pulled over and Jordan came to the driver's window to say "hello." They talked for a minute and then Jordan asked, "Boys, I'm going to have a crew down in Tallulah Gorge at the hydro plant a week from Friday. Would you like to come and take a tour while we're there?"

Leed said, "Sure."

Jordan said, "Ask your dad if he would like to join us."

Leed answered, "OK."

"Well, meet me a week from Friday at 1:00 in the parking lot on the south rim of the gorge by the incline railway cable wheel house." They told their dad when they got home and he was as excited as they were, but tried not to show it.

Leed got to thinking and he figured out that the day they were going down in the gorge to tour the Georgia Power generating complex was also the day he would turn eighteen years old. He thought what a wonderful birthday present to see something that was on the register of engineering feats after its completion in the first part of the century.

The day came and Telford told the boys they didn't have to go to school because of the trip. They worked around the farm, ate lunch and then got in the pickup and drove out to U.S. Highway 441. Their journey took them south along the Tallulah River, over Saw-tooth Bridge, around by the Terorra Power Plant, along the shore of Tallulah Falls Lake, where the road went under the Talluah Falls Railroad's huge steel trestle that crossed the lake and the road in one long span. They went on over the short bridge which crossed a finger of the lake, around to the high bridge that crossed the gorge just below the dam, and on through the town of Talluah Falls.

Highway 441 went along the rim of the gorge by the railroad track, past the look-off, and took them to the turn off to Tallulah Lodge, where the incline railway wheel house was located. They drove around to the parking lot by the wheel house and parked. Jordan was waiting for them and waved them over. As they approached he said, "Happy Birthday, Leed."

Leed shyly answered, "Thank you."

Jordan told them that the incline railway car had gone down into the gorge with a crew about ten minutes earlier and it should be back up in another ten minutes.

Soon the car pulled up to the platform and they got on and gave a signal that they were ready to the operator who was located at the bottom of the gorge. With a slight jostle the car, which was built up on a frame to make it level while its wheels were angled down more than forty-five degrees, started rolling down the steeply in-clined rails.

Leed asked, "That appears to be a three quarter inch cable let-ting us down; what if it broke?"

Jordan said, "Do you see that one inch cable beside it that's not moving?"

Leed answered, "Yes."

"Well there is a brake mechanism on this car. If the cable breaks and the car runs away, the brakes will grab that cable and stop the car, and then we'll have to climb out," grinned Jordan. "Besides that," Jordan continued, "do you see that big rail platform parked above where we got on?"

Leed said, "Yes."

Jordan continued, "Well that platform will bring forty tons down into the gorge."

Leed nodded, indicating his acceptance of the car's safety.

He was surprised at how slowly the cable lowered the car down the rails. It gave Jordan time to point out some items of interest and to talk with Telford. There was still plenty of time for the boys to look around and check out everything. They hunkered down and looked at an angle overhead and saw huge power lines climbing out of and across the gorge to giant steel towers on both sides. The ones to the north brought power from all the other dams and generating complexes to the North as well as feeding Rabun County. The ones to the South fed all the way to Atlanta and the one to the East fed over into South Carolina. To their left were six big pipes that Jordan called penstocks that came out of the rock near the top of the gorge. Jordan told them there was a tunnel that was several thousand feet long that had been cut through solid rock to bring the water around, under the city of Tallulah Falls from Tallulah Falls Lake to the penstocks. Below them was a huge brick building with a lot of windows around the top that housed the generators. The incline railway ended right beside that building. Predominate on both walls of the gorge were cliffs, boulders and very determined trees.

When they arrived at the bottom they stepped out onto concrete that led right to the building. When they entered Benji asked Jordan, "Why is the floor quivering?"

Jordan answered, "They're running four of the hydro-driven generators today." Jordan explained everything as they toured. They saw huge generators sticking up through the floor and then went down to the next floor below where they saw the housings that encased the impellers that were being turned by the force of the water coming through the penstocks. They were turning the generators above, through thick vertical shafts. Leed was awestruck by all of the mechanical wonder before his eyes.

Soon they worked their way up and over to where the big copper bars carried the electricity from the generators through protective ceramic brick passageways, with vent openings for cooling, to the point where they hooked up to the transformers. Here the generated electricity was changed into high voltage to be sent into the North Georgia grid or, if needed, they could send it through the tower lines that crossed the gorge and then went east across Tuga-loo Lake into South Carolina.

Leed felt like he was in a very special place... a place he'd like to work some day, "All that I'd need would be to graduate from Georgia Tech."

Finally they went into the control room where the technicians ran the entire complex there in the gorge as well as coordinating the power generated at the hydro plants at Lake Burton, Seed Lake, Terorra Power Plant, Tugaloo Lake and Yonah Lake. Leed asked one of the operators what he did during a lightning storm in the summer time. He grinned and answered, "I set right here and hun-ker down until all the popping stops, then I reset everything."

They went back outside and walked over to the edge where they could look down to see where the water was boiling out from under the side of the building. Leed thought it was an awesome sight to see that much water appear as the cement quivered under his feet. He followed the water with his eyes to where it joined the water running through the gorge and then on down to where it ran into Tugaloo Lake.

Telford called Leed out of his dream world and said, "We gotta' go." So they all loaded onto the incline rail car and headed up, out of the gorge. As they ascended to the top, Leed thought once again how awesome it would be, someday, to work for a great com-pany like Georgia Power. Back at the wheelhouse parking lot Leed thanked Jordan for such a great birthday present and they got into the pickup and headed home.

Linda had Leed's favorite cake ready and Tommy Hawk showed up at the appointed time and they had a little party to celebrate Leed's coming of age. That night, as he lay in bed with things run-ning through his mind, Leed thought, "I'm now eighteen years old and I don't know what I'm going to do for work or school after I graduate. I don't know where I'm going to move to, I don't have no girl friend or even a good prospect of one, and I don't know what I'm going to do or where I'm going to go when I leave this life. This growing up shore is complicated and it ain't much fun neither!"

One Saturday morning Leed looked outside on the way to breakfast to see a cold rain coming straight down. Telford said, "We ain't going to do much today boys, it's just too nasty out there. I'll do the milkin' and ya'll can do the chores this afternoon and that's about all we'll do today."

After Linda had finished the dishes she walked into the front room with a big ole boiler full of soup beans with a big slab of fat back in them and said, "Boys here's supper fer tonight," as she set the boiler on top of the heater. Leed and Benji did their home work and then Telford pulled out the chess board. He had learned to play while he was away in the army and was pretty good at it. Leed was good at chess too, but for some reason chess made sense to Benji. He was aggressive and you had to watch him close or he'd trap you and holler checkmate before you knew it. It was hard for Telford or Leed to beat him.

That evening Leed and Benji did their chores and then Telford and Leed played a long game of chess while the smell of cooking beans flavored the room with anticipation. Leed walked into the kitchen, while Telford and Benji played one last game. His mom already had the cook stove hot and the frying' pan had been in the oven for a while, heating up with the grease in it. She mixed up the corn meal, eggs and buttermilk and then reached down and picked up the small lard bucket.

Leed realized she was going to make cracklin' bread. She pulled the lid off of the small lard bucket and dipped out a couple of spoons full of cracklin's into the bowl, replaced the lid and set the bucket down. She stirred the cracklin's into the cornmeal batter, got a potholder, opened the oven door and pulled out the hot pan of grease. She poured the hot grease into the bowl, sat the frying pan down on the stove and stirred in the grease, then poured the mixture into the hot pan where it started to fry right then. She slid the pan back into the oven, laid the potholder down and put some more wood into the fire box.

It was the perfect supper for a cold day in the winter. Telford had placed a peck bucket full of water on the heater and all the spare boilers full of water on the wood cook stove to heat. They would all take a bath that night so they wouldn't smell like grandpa at church the next morning. They put one big wash tub in the kitchen for the men to wash in and another in the living room, near the heater, for Linda.

How they took a bath in cold weather was a long-established routine. They would stand in the big wash tub and pour water on themselves with a small boiler used just for that. Then they would soap up with Ivory Soap and a rag and rinse with the boiler, then step out and dry off. Leed was just glad the kitchen was still warm from the cornbread cooking. Sometimes when it was real cold they had to take turns bathing in the living room, because it was too cold to use the kitchen if the old wood range hadn't been heated for a while. In fact, in the wintertime most of the canned goods were kept in the cellar on shelves with old quilts over them to keep them from freezing.

Later that night they all were sitting around the heater in the front room and Telford started turning the knob on the AM Radio. The radio made the funny sounds of tuning until finally Telford brought in the Grand Ole Opry. For the next couple of hours they heard Roy Acuff, Minnie Pearl, Ernest Tubb, Little Jimmy Dickens and even Bill Monroe who played bluegrass. This was a good way to end a long day before they all went to their cold beds and started the ritual of warming up a spot to sleep under all of that cover.

———————————

The next few weeks the boys worked hard at school and at home. It being wintertime added heavy to the chores they had to do around the house each evening. They had to feed fodder, hay and crushed corn to the mules and cows, slop the hogs, feed the chickens crushed corn and all of the normal things that they did all year. But on top of that, they had to keep the porch stacked with wood for the heater, keep stove wood in a bucket and a big box just inside the kitchen. Plus they had to split rich pine lighter and kindling for both the heater and the wood cook stove. This took until dark about every night. About every week or two they had to take the ashes out of the heater and go out and spread them in the garden.

Then later in the evening they studied while their dad and mom would read the Bible. About the only thing that broke up the routine was the AM station that their mom listened to. At night when the clear AM stations would crank their power up as the small AM stations went off the air, they could hear country music, gospel music and sometimes bluegrass music for a little while between homework and bed. The whole family liked to gather and listen to the radio or the record player in the evening and relax after everything was done.

Their dad was still cutting logs and the boys would help him load logs on Saturday. Logging was hard work at any time, but it was real tough in the wintertime. Their fingers always seemed to hurt from the cold, even if they had gloves on. And their ears would stay cold, unless they had a stocking hat or a hat with ear flaps. It seemed like it was muddy all the time and the logs were cold, wet, muddy and slick which made them hard to roll up onto the truck. When it got real cold, the logs would freeze to the ground and they had to break them loose with a mule or the truck. Then they would have to take an axe, after they had rolled them over, and chop the big skirts of mud off which were still frozen to the log.

The way they loaded all but the biggest logs, which they needed the mules to help with, was to cut three or four poles to support the log and lay them up on the side of the truck after they dropped the standards off that side. The poles were cut long and the truck was parked in a low spot to make as low a slope as possible to roll the logs up. Telford and the boys would then take two cant hooks and lay their ends up on the side of the log and drop the hinged cant down and stick the hook into the bark of the log. Then Telford would pick up on the handle of one cant hook and the boys would pick up on the handle of the other one. They would roll the log almost a quarter turn and the boys would hold the log there while their dad caught another hold. Then he would hold the log while they caught another hold and they would go another quarter turn. This was slow but they could load a big log this way.

The trouble came when they had to roll a butt-cut log up the ramp. A butt-cut was the first cut of the log, just above the ground, and was cone shaped so one end would get ahead of the other as they rolled it up the poles. When that happened, they had to hold the small end up hill and slide the big end back down hill a little bit. This would really tire Telford and the boys out, so they usually put the butt-cuts on first while they were fresh. They loaded a load of logs about every Saturday and Telford would take them to the mill on Monday. He would then cut and drag during the week to have another load ready for the next week, so they would have money to live off of through the long hard winter.

Leed struggled mightily through the winter, not talking much at school or at home; he just worked and studied. His interest in the engineering books and working out problems was about all that kept him going. He didn't even scoot board when Benji and Tommy Hawk went. Finally it got on toward the beginning of spring, but with just a little over two weeks of winter left, it was still dark, cold and grey just like Leed had become.

That Saturday they loaded logs as usual and it was cold. When they got home Leed didn't feel good so he went to bed. The next morning his mom checked on him and he had a high fever and was chilling. She went into the living room and made him a bed in there. After she moved him, she went into the kitchen and said with a mother's concern, "Telford, I think Leed has the flu. You and Benji go on to church and I'll stay here and take care of him. And have everyone pray for him at church; you know how many people die from influenza every year.

His mom stayed close and watched Leed until his fever broke on Tuesday. She would sit beside him and feed him soup she had made and give him water. And when he was asleep she would pray over him. When his fever broke she praised the Lord and finally got a good night's sleep. Leed finally got his strength back and went back to school on Thursday.

Early the next week Telford got a letter in the mail. After supper he read it and then just sat and studied a long time. Finally

137

Linda asked, with concern, "What's wrong, Telford?"

Telford answered, "You remember my first cousin Larry, on my mom's side, from down at Clarkesville, that killed a feller? It was a few years ago. It was over that fellers wife." She said, "Yes." Telford continued, "Well, Uncle Bill wrote that Larry's going to the electric chair Thursday down in Jackson. He said that Larry won't listen to him and he wants me to go down and try to talk some sense into him, before he goes to hell."

Leed, who had been listening, said before he thought, "Are you going to go, dad?"

Telford thought a minute and said, "Son, if you'll go with me I'll go!" Leed caught by surprise thought for just a second and then replied, "I'll go!"

The next day Telford called the warden and got permission to talk to Larry on Thursday prior to the execution. But they had to be there at least one hour before the scheduled execution at 1:00 p.m. The trip to Jackson took about five hours, so they left at six in the morning so they would be there in plenty of time. On the way down they stopped at a diner and got a quick breakfast and a cup of coffee and hit the road again. As they rode, Leed finally got the courage to ask his dad what Larry had done.

Telford told him, "Well Larry got to seeing the wife of a man that was working evening shift and he fell for her; and I don't see why, for she was a sorry one. But anyway, one night the feller got sick and come home from work early and caught Larry, in his home, with his wife and a fight broke out. They ended up in the kitchen and Larry, in the heat of the moment, grabbed a knife off of the table and stabbed him to death. He got the death sentence and has been in jail for several years waiting on his death sentence to be carried out."

"Oh!" was all that Leed could get out. But his thoughts were running wild, "If Larry is going to die today, what is he thinking? Is he ready to go? Where will he go? How will he take this day? Does he regret what he did? Has he apologized, repented or asked for forgiveness, of anyone?" And the question that stayed with Leed on down the road was, "Where will Larry be at the end of this day?"

When they arrived, the guard called the warden and made sure that they had permission to be there for the execution, before he would allow them in. He then searched them and allowed them to enter. As they walked along the stone and concrete walls, Leed felt very uneasy and he had to talk to himself to keep from running. The cold, uneasy feeling got worse every time the steel bar doors slammed with great finality behind them. When they reached death row the guard told Telford that they had fifteen minutes to talk with Larry before the preacher would talk with him.

When they arrived at Larry's cell Telford introduced Leed to Larry and then Leed backed out into the hall with the guard as his dad had instructed. Leed could hear his dad trying to talk to Larry about his need for Jesus. But all Larry did was keep asking about the woman whose husband he had killed.

"Do you ever see her, Telford, does she ever ask about me? Where's she at now, what's she doing?"

Finally Telford shouted, "Larry, she don't care about you, she's married to some feller and living down in Gainesville now and has been for some time!"

He answered with a raised voice, "No! It can't be true, you're lyin'!"

Telford said, "No I ain't lying, Larry. Look at me. You're less than an hour from dying and going out into eternity on your on, and you ain't ready! Will you please listen to me?"

With a growing terror in his voice, Larry begged, "I got to see her, Telford; will you take me to see her? Will you?" The guard, sensing trouble, opened the door and asked Telford to step out. As Telford stepped through the door, Larry was still pleading, "Telford take me to see her, now Telford, now!" Telford made one last plea, "Jesus is waiting on you to call on Him Larry, call on Him, please."

Then the guard said, "Sorry your time's up; you have to go down to the viewing room." Telford wiped his eyes as he and Leed walked down the hall to a room with windows that looked into where the electric chair was. As Telford stood there with his head down, Leed became very anxious when he thought about how much his spiritual situation was like Larry's.

Finally the Warden came in and talked to Telford for just a moment and said, "It won't be long now." Telford looked at the warden and said, "Thank you for allowing us to come see Larry today, but I don't want to watch him go to hell, so we're going to leave." The warden nodded his head and motioned for a guard to escort them out. As they made their way back through the steel bar gates and along the rock and concrete walls, the lights suddenly dimmed, came back bright and then dimmed again. With the first dimming Telford stopped and put his hand on the wall and steadied himself until after the second dimming. Then he headed out with his head hung low, walking like he was in pain.

Once outside they went straight to the car and headed home. Telford never spoke to Leed during the five hour ride back to Rabun County, but Leed could tell he was praying inside most of the way, so he didn't say anything either. Leed knew that his dad, who loved him so very much, was praying for him so he wouldn't end up in the same state as Larry now found himself in.

CHAPTER 15

SPRING

The next week winter died on out and spring time arrived. But in the mountains the first few weeks of spring can be a whole lot like winter; nevertheless things were starting to thaw out. The daffodils and jonquils had been blooming for a while and were about gone, as were the yellow bells. The grass was greening up and the chickens were starting to lay good again, so things were a looking better all the time.

Then came the one day that really said spring was here. The first day of trout season was on the last day of March every year, and if it came on a weekday, they let school out, because everybody was going fishing anyway. This year March thirty-first fell on a Wednesday, so Leed and Benji had a trip planned. They had two Prince Albert cans full of worms they had dug out behind the hog pen and were anxious to go. Their dad would drop them off at the bridge where U.S. 441 crosses Tiger Creek just below the big curved train trestle and just above the junction with Stonewall Creek. Then they would wade and fish down Tiger Creek about 100 yards to Stonewall Creek, and then wade and fish back up Stonewall Creek about a mile or two to Stonewall Falls, where Telford would pick them up that evening.

They fished hard and kept only the trout that were about twelve inches long or longer and they both had their limit by the time they got to the falls. Benji had a beautiful eighteen-inch rainbow he caught below one of the bridges, near where the old dinky line railroad bed ran along the creek. Georgia Power had the dinky line laid up Stonewall, along by possum ridge, through the gap, across

Sawmill Creek, across Bridge Creek and around to the Tallulah River. It was used to haul in cement, steel and supplies back when they built Burton Dam. When they reached the falls they sat on the big rocks, in the cool shade until their dad came. Back at home they cleaned the fish and had a big trout supper.

Telford and his family put in a joint garden with Jeremiah and Ruby, as much to help them as for their own good. This made for a busy spring because Grandpa liked a big garden. The next few weeks were real busy just like the last couple had been. The early taters, peas and greens were already in, now it was time to plant the big patch of taters for digging in the fall and the beans had to go in on Good Friday. The eating corn and the field corn would soon go in and the tomato plants would go in later in May, because there was always a chance of frost in Rabun County up into the middle of May.

Leed really listened to Preacher Bill on Easter Sunday. When he read in Luke 22:33 where Peter said that he would go to prison or even death with Jesus, but Jesus told him in the next verse that he was about to deny him three times. Then he read on in Luke, chapter 22 and verses 54 through 60 how, when Jesus was in the high priest's house under arrest, Peter, one of Jesus' own disciples, did deny him, not once but three times. It was just like Jesus had said. Then in verses 61 and 62, Peter remembered Jesus' words and ran and cried bitterly.

Leed thought, "Maybe its just part of a human being to reject the very One who has come to help you and is the only One who can help you." Then he thought, "That's not very smart on our part though, but how do you get to know this very One that you have been rejecting?" At the invitation, he wanted to, but couldn't go forward, even though he tried; he didn't know what held him back. This weighed heavy on him that week, but for the first time in a long time he felt like there was hope, if he could just figure out how to get to God.

A varmint had been coming around, chasing and killing chickens for about a week. Grandpa was on edge, worried about losing eggs and later on, fried chicken. On Tuesday night before he and Ruby went to bed, he made sure old Betsy, his faithful muzzle loading rifle, was loaded, at half cock and capped. About eleven o'clock the chickens started raising a ruckus out at the hen house. It woke Grandpa so he got up, slid his boots on while sitting on the side of the bed, went through the door into the front room, spun and reached above the bedroom door and grabbed old Betsy.

As he headed for the door, Ruby, who had gotten up, demanded, "Jeremiah, you ain't got no clothes on, where you goin'?" "Woman, I got my union suit on and that's good enough," he answered. She said, "But your rear flap has only one button and part of your behind is showing!" He snorted, "Ain't nobody but that varmint out there nohow." And he stepped out the door and headed for the henhouse.

As he went behind the house he full cocked the gun and started up the hill. The moon was shining bright and he could see real good. He looked up toward the hen house and didn't see anything. Then he looked back toward the house and thought, "Where's that sorry dog at? If he was a do'in his job, then I wouldn't have to be out here." Jeremiah started slipping along real slow and thinking to himself, "That varmint ain't got no chance with a crack shot like me coming after him! His pelt is mine!"

As Grandpa slipped along, he didn't notice that the sorry dog had finally come out from under the floor, had caught up and was now slipping right along behind him. As Grandpa took a step so did the sorry hound. When he stopped, the hound stopped. When he crouched and slipped forward, the flea bitten silhouette was right behind him. Finally he eased up to the henhouse and thought, "That varmint ain't run yet, he must still be in there. I've got 'em!" Grandpa bent over, used the muzzle of the rifle to ease the door of the henhouse open, and slipped his head inside of the low roofed henhouse.

144

Now all this put too much strain on his old union suit and it popped the one remaining button off the flap, which allowed the flap to fall down and expose him right there in the bright moon light. That sorry dog was right behind him and took immediate interest in the situation. The hound eased forward, sniffing, and stuck his cold nose right against what was exposed. Every muscle in Grandpa's body tightened and he let out a squall like a painter, as the cold nose found its mark. He jerked up and hit his head on the tin roof of the hen house and made a big racket. But that racket wasn't nearly as loud as the report of the muzzle-loading rifle going off, as it shot a hole right through the roof of the henhouse.

Smoke from the rifle billowed everywhere as Grandpa fell to his knees, addled and wondering where he was. That sorry dog, realizing that there was way too much action at the hen house, headed for his place under the porch as fast as a rabbit; Grandpa never knew what got him. After he got his wits about himself, Grandpa ran to the house and almost out of breath, told his wife, "Ruby, I been attackted by a bugger and he run and got away! He was on me before I nowed it and I must've missed him! I thank he come at me from behind. Yeah, that's how he got me, from behind!"

Ruby just shook her head and said, "Jeremiah if you're going back outside you better put your britches on."

The next morning Jeremiah was up at Telford's before breakfast telling everybody about his run-in with the bugger the night before, and showing them the cut on his head from the hen house.

Benji said, "We heard you shooting, Grandpa. We figured you was after something." They all heard the bugger story for the next month, before Grandpa finally let it rest.

Ronnie and Lonnie had gone down to Toccoa before Christmas and hired a man that their dad had known to build them a still. The man worked for a sheet metal company and was real good at working with sheet copper. He told them that he was busy and to come back in three or four months and he would have it, so they figgered it was ready by now.

On Saturday they drove down to Toccoa, paid the feller, loaded the still in the old pickup and hid it under a tarp to haul it back. But it still looked awful suspicious, so they got worried and crossed the river there at Prather's covered bridge and drove up the back roads in South Carolina. They went up by Black Mountain, over to Highway 76 and then headed west through Long Creek and back into Georgia, taking the back roads to their house. They went straight to the river and put it in a johnboat they had and floated it down the river to a still-house that they had fixed back in the winter that was up a branch on the back side of Crumley Mountain. They felt it was a place that they wouldn't get caught. After they unloaded the still, they let the johnboat go because there was a big sycamore that had fallen halfway across the river in the bend down stream that would trap the boat until they drove around the mountain and down stream to get it. The boat would be needed to bring the corn, sugar and jars in and to carry the cases of fruit jars full of liquor out. They got home tired but proud. They were almost back in business.

Monday evening after school, Ronnie and Lonnie got out of the old truck after school and were standing out in the yard talking before they went in the house. Jeff came running from the barn, straight to Lonnie, who reached down to pet his friend, "Hey my buddy, how are ye, did'ja miss me today?"

Ronnie growled, "Listen, we'll have to go get sugar in the morning before school so we gotta' get up early, so come on, let's eat supper!"

Ronnie and Lonnie wallowed around in bed the next morning just like they always did and didn't leave for the store as early as they wanted too. Lonnie said, "We can't get the sugar, we slept too late."

"Bull," answered Ronnie, "we're businessmen and business comes first!" After driving around behind the store, they loaded the bales of sugar they'd bought in the back of the truck, covered their cargo with a tarp and drove to school.

They were almost an hour late when they walked in and from the steely look on Mrs. Stancil's narrow face, Ronnie knew she wasn't happy. She firmly inquired, "Where have you boys been?"

Ronnie stuttered out a lie, "We had a flat tar!"

Mrs. Stancil didn't look convinced, so as she reached to her desk for paper, as she said, "Well, while you were out, you boys missed a test and I'm going to let you make it up. Now Ronnie, you get in the desk in that corner and Lonnie you get in the desk back in that corner." They both looked suspicious, but went to the desks as directed. After they sat down she brought them each a piece of paper and a sharp pencil she pulled from her gray hair that was pulled into a tight bun on her head. Then, with a forming smile and a firm look of control, she said, "There will be no talking during this test. Now each of you write down which tire was flat!" Ronnie looked worried and disgusted at the same time, while Lonnie looked as lost as he usually did when he took a test.

She waited for a couple of minutes until they were finished writing, and walked over and picked up Ronnie's paper and read, "The right rear. Good, Ronnie, now let's see what your brother has written?" She walked over and picked up Lonnie's paper and turned livid as she read aloud, "The one that didn't have no air in it." She looked at Lonnie a long second, as her narrow features seem to sharpen, and asked in an angry tone, "Are you ignorant and apathetic?"

Lonnie, thinking this was still part of the test and knowing he didn't know the right answer, responded, "I don't know and I don't keer." The whole class laughed out loud and Lonnie thought that he had finally given the right answer to something and grinned, proud of himself.

Mrs. Stancil was real mad and she screamed for everyone to be quiet and told Ronnie and Lonnie to turn their desks toward each corner in the back of the room and not to look out, or say anything until lunch.

Grandpa's sow had pigs a while back and he had asked the boys to come down on Thursday evening and help him cut them. Ruby had promised to feed the boys supper also. As Leed and Benji walked down to their Grandpa's, Benji asked, "Why does grandpa cut almost everything for?"

Leed pondered a second, "Well you know his sayin', 'on the

farm when something gets out of line, you cut it'. And he also says that cutting pigs when they're young makes the meat better when they are older, and cutting tom cats keeps them close around to catch rats."

Benji answered, "You know, I wonder about that one, most of the time when you cut a cat they get sorry and just lay around and won't catch nothing."

"Well he's got his knife sharp and he's gonna cut something so we better help him," smiled Leed.

When they got there Jeremiah was already at the barn ready to go. He fed the sow and the boys started catching the pigs. When Leed and Benji would catch a boy pig, they would take turns laying the pig over the top plank on the stall with its butt up in the air. They would hold its legs apart and grandpa would make short work of the pig's masculinity and when they set it down it was officially a barr, not a boar. As the pigs ran back to their mom they would go, "runt, runt, runt," and Jeremiah would say, "Pigs is the smartest animals on the farm; just listen to 'em, they knows they's ruint because they keep tellin' it on the way back to their mammy, I'm ruint, ruint, ruint."

After they got through with the pigs, grandpa asked the boys, "Can ya'll help me by throwing down some hay from the loft?" They answered, "Sure." He said, "Well, be keerful then, its getting dark. I'll fill the lantern with kerosene oil then, and light it up so ya'll can see."

When they got through they went into the house, washed up and sat down to eat. Ruby set out a gallon of sweet milk, a big cake of cornbread and a big boiler full of squirrel and dumplings. While Grandma was filling up the reused Bama jelly glasses with milk, Jeremiah admitted, "Them squirrels was a getting into the corn crib and I had to shoot em!"

"Sure Grandpa," Benji grinned. As Ruby dipped out a bunch of squirrel and dumplings into the boy's plates, Leed and Benji looked apprehensively at the squirrels that seemed to be looking back at them with their heads still attached. The boys looked at each other and kind of wished that they had passed on supper. The dumplings were good but the dark gray meat of a squirrel is a long way from the beautiful pink and white meat of a rabbit. The boys left the heads alone while Grandpa ate his first. He would take the back of a spoon and crack their head open like a nut and eat the brains out with the spoon. Both Leed and Benji donated their squirrel heads to Grandpa who was happy to get them.

After supper Jeremiah told the boys, "Carry the kerosene lantern on the way back home tonight so no mad dog won't get'che, alright!" The boys agreed and told their grandparents good night.

As they walked home Benji asked Leed, "Why is all the old people scared of mad dogs fer, I ain't never even seen one?"

Leed answered, "Well, when they was growin' up there weren't no cure for rabies, so they was real cautious about any unusual acting dog or other animal. Dad said that when he was a boy, just the shout of 'mad dog,' when a bunch of people was walking, was enough to start a stampede."

"Boy I hope we don't meet one tonight!" worried Benji.

On Saturday Ronnie and Lonnie went and retrieved the johnboat and hauled it back around the mountain. Then they floated the sugar and corn down and fixed the mash barrels so they could make a run the next Saturday. They needed to make some money.

CHAPTER 16 TRAGEDY

On Thursday the boys had agreed to take the lantern and the chain saw back to Jeremiah's house and help him cut a bee tree he'd found. Bee trees are best cut at night, so the boys said they would be there late. This was deliberate to avoid any chance that Grandma might have the other dark meat for supper! As far as Leed and Benji were concerned, groundhog wasn't any better than squirrel.

They drove the pickup to haul the big McCullough two-man bow saw with them, which was the only chain saw they had, but that was all the chain saw you needed when you log. As they pulled up to Grandpa's yard, a 1935 Chevrolet pickup was sitting in the yard. Leed said, "I wonder who that is?" When they got out they found out it was someone who come to buy some tame turkeys from Grandpa. He raised and sold turkeys for what he called easy retirement money.

They walked out back where Grandpa was getting ready to bring some turkeys down out of the tree where they roosted. The way he had figured out to get just the turkey that he wanted to sell was pretty ingenious. He would wrap aluminum foil around the back of his kerosene oil lamp to throw all the light one way. Then he would have someone hold the lantern at an angle, where he could see up into the tree. With a long round pole he would push against the breast of the turkey he had picked out. As he slowly pushed the turkey back into the dark, the big, awkward bird would get off balance, start flopping his wings and, in desperation, reach up with his feet and grab a hold of the pole. Then Grandpa would just lower the flopping turkey down to the ground with the pole, where a helper would grab the turkey by the legs and sack him.

After they had brought down three turkeys from one tree for the man, he wanted two more young ones. So they moved over to the next tree and Benji held the kerosene lantern back so they could see the turkeys in that tree. Jeremiah was looking straight up at the turkeys that were right over his head. He was a pointing and saying, "Now that'ns fer sale and that'ns fer sale and that'ns fer sale." All of a sudden he went to sputtering, gagging and spitting all over the ground. After he went to the well and washed his mouth out with a couple of dippers full of water, he finally got his wits back about him. He came back to where everyone was standing and said, "Well now, I want'cha to know, if'n I hadn't a had my mouth open, that turkey would'a pooped right in my face!" Everybody chuckled and they finished the turkey sale without further ado.

After the man left with the turkeys, Leed got the chainsaw and Benji carried the lantern, an axe and bow saw, while Jeremiah got a bee hive super, which is the removable top portion of a bee hive where the bees store the honey and a cap to put over the super. He also had a bunch of rags to seal between the square super and the round tree trunk that the hive was in, because they wouldn't match after they cut the hive section out of the tree.

After they found the bee tree that Jeremiah had located and marked, they sawed it down and quickly stuffed a rag into the hole, in the hollow log, that the bees went in and out through. This allowed Leed to saw through the tree about four feet below the hole to make sure they got most of the hive and honey. Then he cut the tree off just above the hole in the hollow tree and Benji stuffed the upper end with rags to keep the bees in. Jeremiah told Leed to cut off about a foot of the tree below the first cut, because they could see a lot of honey oozing out there. The hive was bigger and went deeper than they thought.

When Leed cut off the one foot piece full of honey, Jeremiah, who had a great love for honey, immediately split it open and run his hand in and got a big handful of honeycomb and went and sat down on the log and started eating. After about two or three minutes, Benji walked over with the lantern and asked Jeremiah if the honey was good.

He smacked, "Yeah, its good, but it tastes kinda funny." Benji

153

held the lantern closer and asked, "What's that white stuff running down your chin Grandpa?" Jeremiah looked real funny and said, "Hold that light right cheer!" and stuck the honeycomb he was eating right up to the lantern. The light revealed that when Jeremiah had carved out a piece of honey comb to eat, he had gotten the comb right at the edge of where the honey storage ended and the larvae started. As he had been eating back and forth he was eating honey, then larvae.

Benji looked amusingly at Jeremiah and asked, "You gonna be alright Grandpa?" Jeremiah answered, "Well I thank so, it was really kind of good. Besides that, bream really thank that them larvae is good."

When Jeremiah stood back up they finished the job by standing the hive section of tree up, jerking the rags out of the top and then capping it with the super and the lid. They quickly sealed around the super and the log, with the rags, where they didn't fit good on the corners. After they propped some sticks against the sides of the hive to keep it from tipping over, they got everything back and Benji pulled the rag out of the hole and the new hive was in business. As they headed back to the house, Jeremiah said, "We got that ready just in time for them to start making good, light colored, summer honey out of sourwood and corn tassels. The boys grinned and talked on the way home about how much fun it was to be around Grandpa.

That Saturday Ronnie and Lonnie brought in several cases of fruit jars and made a real good run. The new still was worth the money they had to pay for a good copper outfit like this. They carried the boxes of fruit jars full of white liquor down and loaded the johnboat, then Ronnie eased down the river while Lonnie walked back upstream and got the pickup. They loaded the cases of jars in the good pickup their mom had loaned them so they could go to Gainesville and deliver the liquor the next day. She knew that good money was coming.

They were in full swing now and Ronnie decided to start keeping a few jars back for local sell out of each run, because he knew he could get more per jar for one jar at a time than for cases at a time. His dad never would do that saying that was a good way to get caught, but Ronnie was braver, or maybe just more stupid, than his dad.

Monday was Benji's birthday, he was seventeen. Since he was nearly grown they just had Tommy Hawk over and had his favorite, not a cake but Chocolate gravy, biscuits and butter. That night Telford and Linda talked about how their kids were all about grown up now and how much Leed wanted to go to college in Atlanta.

Linda asked, "Telford isn't there some way we can send him to Georgia Tech? I think he would make a great engineer."

Telford just shook his head and said, "I want to as much as you but we just don't have that kind of money." "Well, when are you going to tell him then?" she asked.

Telford mused a moment and said, "I guess when school is out later this month. He'll be a man then and he can decide what he wants to do." Linda wiped back a tear and hugged Telford.

The next week on Thursday Leed went over to Jordan Laycock's house to study and after they had worked about forty-five minutes, Jordan looked at Leed and said, "I got your grades from school and took them to Georgia Tech on my last trip to Atlanta, just like we talked about."

"Thanks," Leed said, and meant it.

Jordan continued, "Well I showed them to Mr. Lawrence, the head of admissions, and I also told him about our studies here at my house. He said you could get into Georgia Tech with no problem, with your grades plus the work we've done together."

"That sounds good, Mr. Laycock, but I just don't think that my parents will have that kind of money to send me there to school. I wish that I could work my way through, but I can't make that kind

of money workin' full time, much less going to school and studying all at the same time." Leed replied, his low sprit evident in his
voice.

"Well, why don't you ask your parents when you get home tonight and let me know what they say?" asked Jordan.

Leed said with an appreciative tone, "I will, Mr. Laycock, and
thank you for working so hard to teach me and help me."

When Leed arrived home his mom and dad were sitting in the
front room listening to the radio. He came in and sat down and
hung his head. His mom looked at him for a long minute, turned
off the radio and asked, "Are you alright, son?"

Leed answered, "Yeah, Mr. Laycock talked to Georgia Tech and
they said that I could shore enough get in, if I had the registration
fee."

Then Telford said, "Well son, we have the registration fee, but
what we don't have is the room and board and tuition that Jordan
talked about. I'm sorry son, we were going to tell you next week
when you got out of school, but we just can't send you to college."
Leed hung his head for a long while as his mom wiped a tear from
her eye.

Leed didn't sleep well that night. He found out how hard it
is to let a dream die. He thought about where he might get a job.
When people graduated from Rabun County High School they either moved to some city, or they farmed, logged, made liquor, or
took a public job in Clayton. There weren't many jobs there though,
and they didn't pay very well either. Sometimes jobs came open
working for the U.S. Forest Service or the Georgia Game and Fish
Department. And every now and then a man could get a job with
the best company to work for in Rabun County. If you could ever
get on one of the Georgia Power line crews or get a job at one of the
dams, you had a great job for life. Those jobs are really sought after
and hard to get though. Leed thought, "I guess I will have to leave
my beloved, Rabun County, the only home I know, if I want to have
a decent job." This thought depressed him until he finally drifted
off to sleep.

The weekend passed and Leed found himself in his last week of school. He always liked school and learning because he was good at it. It was going to be tough leaving school and getting a job because there was so much more that Leed wanted to learn. He also wanted to get a job that required him to use his brain and that would be a challenge to him. He thought of what could have been.

Graduation was Friday night and everybody came. Even Jeremiah cleaned up and took a bath for the occasion. Leed was third in his class behind two girls, and he was glad because he sure didn't want to give a speech. Ronnie and Lonnie both graduated too, because their mom wouldn't let them quit and the teachers passed them to get rid of them. Now they really thought they were something when they got their names called out and received their diplomas. It was hot, though, and everybody was glad when it was over.

Outside, Leed's parents and grandparents were talking with everyone they met, so Leed stepped out toward where the cars were parked. He looked out in the parking lot and saw Ronnie and Furlon Stancil standing by the open door of Ronnie's old truck. Ronnie reached in on the seat of the truck and pulled out a brown paper sack that looked about the right size to have a quart fruit jar in it. He handed the sack with what Leed suspected were illicit contents in it to Furlon, who in turn handed him some money and they said some words. Then Furlon went over to where his buddy, Randall Lee, was waiting and they got in Furlon's hot rod Ford and took off. Leed just shook his head and thought "Ronnie is just like his dad." Leed didn't even go to town that night, but just went home with his folks.

The next morning the boys slept in because Telford had to go to town to get some supplies to change oil in the trucks. When he got back, Leed and Benji were in the kitchen eating sausage, eggs and biscuits, leftover from breakfast in the warmer over the top of the wood cook stove. Telford walked in and said, "Boys, I've got bad news for you! Furlon Stancil and Randall Lee were killed in a car wreck late last night!"

Leed was shocked and asked, "What happened?"

"Well," Telford answered, "they was just a flying down the Arrendale Stretch there below Tiger on U.S. 441 and didn't let off a bit when they started into the curves. They finally ran out of the road and hit the bank and started flipping and flipped off in the branch there next to the little spring house across the road from the cane patch on Tiger Creek."

"Why didn't they let off?" asked Benji.

Telford answered, "The deputy said that they was dead when he arrived, but they stunk like white liquor, and he found a quart jar busted into pieces all over the floor board. I guess Furlon was too drunk to think."

"That's the liquor that Furlon bought from Ronnie and it killed them. Ronnie has blame in this," Leed judged in his heart.

Neither Leed nor Benji could finish their breakfast, so they went out on the porch. Leed was smoldering and said to Benji, "I saw Ronnie sell a jar of white liquor to Furlon last night after the graduation!"

"You shore?" asked Benji.

"Yeah, I saw it clear!" "We should go tell dad!" exclaimed Benji.

"Yeah we should tell the Sheriff too! But here in the mountains, we'd be shunned if we did that. Benji, just let me think about this one, I'm the one that seen Ronnie hand him that jar." Leed said, as his eyes narrowed.

Then Benji said, thinking out loud, "Yeah I guess our raisen' does have its limitations."

The next morning after breakfast, Leed told his dad that he wouldn't be going to church because he felt too bad about Furlon and Randall. Telford looked at him and said, "Son, I feel bad about this too, but I'm going to church anyway and as long as you live in my house you're going too, do you understand?" Leed hung his head and said, "Yes sir!"

Leed sat quietly through church wondering where Furlon and Randall were now that they had left this world. Then he got to thinking; everybody dies some time and they only have now, here in time, to get ready to die. This is our, my one opportunity to prepare for eternity. About that time Leed was brought back from his thoughts by the verse that Preacher Bill was reading. It was Romans 6:23 and this was what he read: "For the wages of sin is death; but the gift of God is eternal life through Jesus Christ our Lord."

Leed thought about how he knew himself and that he had lied before and he knew how he thought about girls sometimes, and he knew what the Bible said about those things. No doubt this meant one thing: he was a sinner. This meant his wages or payment due was death. But the verse went on and said that eternal life was a gift from God. Leed wondered, "How do you get this gift?" but the anger about his friends' untimely deaths came burning back, and he couldn't think about this gift clearly.

The next day he went to Furlon's funeral with Benji and Tommy Hawk. It was a sad sight and the preacher didn't have much to say about heaven when he was a talking about Furlon. It didn't last long and neither did Randall's funeral the next day. Two funerals made for a long week for everyone.

Jordan Laycock had a scheduled meeting at the Georgia Power headquarters in Atlanta for the next week. He knew Frank Wheeler the President of Georgia Power personally, so he called and set up a meeting with him for the following Tuesday.

After Jordan had finished his scheduled meeting, he went to the president's office and waited. When the secretary showed him in, he exchanged pleasantries with Frank and got right down to business. "Frank you told me last year that you want to hire the best engineers for Georgia Power, but the best Georgia Tech engineering graduates seem to take jobs out of state with companies outside of the utility industry, because the utility industry isn't as attractive to them."

Frank said, "That's right, Jordan. What have you got in mind?"

Jordan continued, "Well Frank, there's a fine young man up in

Rabun County that is smart as a whip and has the grades to prove it. Plus, I've been working with him for two years now. The problem is, his family doesn't have the money to send him to Tech." "Do you think Tech would take him?" asked Frank. Jordan answered, "Yes, I've already shown his grades to Mr. Lawrence and they would love to have a bright young man like that."

Frank mused for a few seconds and said, "OK, so where do we come into play here as a company? Are you suggesting we give money away?"

Jordan grinned, "Not exactly. But I do have an idea. What if we finance, or invest in the boy's education, and in return, he has to go to work for Georgia Power after he graduates, at normal pay, and has to stay with us for at least two years for every year of schooling we pay for." Jordan paused to gauge the president's reactions. "And he has to pay back his school bill during those years so we can have it for another student."

"That's interesting Jordan. What else do you have in that head of yours?" Frank asked.

Jordan on a roll now went on, "Well, I think if someone works for a good company like Georgia Power for eight years they will definitely stay. This will be a good way to get good, long term engineers and we can hand pick them this way to suit our needs and to guarantee their quality."

Frank, really interested said, "So, you're contemplating an entirely new program for Georgia Power?"

Jordan smiled and nodded. He continued, "And that isn't all. Since we want to acclimate the students to Georgia Power as soon and as completely as possible, we can require that they work for an hourly wage each summer while they are in school and we can send them out to one of the regional offices for training in those areas where we need engineers. This summer work would be a plus to the young engineers to give them some hands-on experience, plus book and spending money too."

Frank smiled and said, "When do you need to know about this to get your young man in Tech?"

Jordan thought a minute and answered, "Probably in the next couple of weeks so Tech can get the paper-work done."

Frank finished, "Well I need to talk to a few people around here, but I should have you an answer by next week." "Thanks," said Jordan and stuck his hand out for a parting handshake.

Jordan went by Georgia Tech after he left the Georgia Power headquarters and found Mr. Lawrence to fill him in on the details of the plan. Mr. Lawrence was excited about the possibility of Leed coming to Georgia Tech that fall. He especially liked the idea of a new program to help smart kids without the resources to be able to come to Tech in the future. The fact that this program would provide summer jobs in an engineering environment pleased him also. While he was there, Jordan obtained all the papers needed to apply at Georgia Tech.

CHAPTER 17

GOOD NEWS

Leed spent that week really thinking about God. He found himself continually asking, "Where do you go when you die? What happens to your soul?" He understood his soul was that part inside of him that does the thinking and wondering and even praying, which he was trying to do now. He was asking God, "Where are You; how do I get to You, how do I get to know You?"

On Friday evening everybody was gone again. Benji and Tommy Hawk went to the drive-in and his mom and dad went to Hiawassee to her sisters. Leed just stayed at home. He thought about going to the cliff again, but, "No" he thought, that was too depressing and he might just jump off of the cliff if he went there.

Finally, as he sat in the front room on the edge of the couch with his head in his hands, he looked up and saw his dad's Bible on the little table, by the big soft chair. He just looked for a long minute and then got up and went to the big chair, sat down and picked up the Bible.

Leed bowed his head and asked a simple prayer, "God, please help me; show me the way?" He opened the Bible and looked through it, reading verses as he went. He was thinking, "I shore would like to get some answers to my questions." He flipped toward the back of the Bible and started slowing down in Acts, scanning the verses. Leed was a very fast reader and could take a lot from a page in a hurry. All of a sudden his eyes caught the word heaven. In Acts 7:49 he read, "Heaven is my throne and earth is my foot stool: what house will ye build me? saith the Lord: or what is the place of my rest?" "Well thank you God, there is the answer to one of my questions, 'Where are you? Maybe I can find out how to get to God if I keep reading," he thought.

He read all around in that area of the Bible for a while, when all of a sudden he came across John 17:3, and he read, "And this is life eternal, that they might know thee, the only true God, and Jesus Christ, whom thou hast sent." He read it over and over again and finally, he thought, "This is defining eternal life, which must mean the same thing as being saved, as knowing God, and also as knowing Jesus Christ whom God has sent." "So being saved is knowing Jesus Christ," Leed thought. "Wow, that can't be too hard; in fact, that don't make no sense! It's too easy! I figured going to heaven would be tough and take a lot of work. This Bible study'n is different than studying books," and he closed the Bible.

Sunday morning came and Leed, while he was in the car on the way to church, asked God to show him the truth. As they were getting out of the car, Preacher Bill rode up on his horse, got off, tied him to the hitching rail, reached in the saddle bag and got out his Bible and notes. He turned and shook hands with Telford and the boys and they all walked into the church.

After Sunday School and a brief break, the morning worship service began. After the singing was over, Preacher Bill got up and started right into preaching the Bible. "Today," he said, "I'm going to teach you about sin, how it started, how it spread down to each of us, and what to do about it. Turn to Romans chapter five and verse twelve. 'Wherefore as by one man sin entered into the world, and death by sin; and so death passed upon all men, for that all have sinned:' Now, most of you ain't young'uns, so you know that this verse is talking about Adam's sin in the Garden of Eden and how it caused death. It means spiritual death, which is separation from God. And it goes on to tell us that death spread to all men. We inherit it from our fathers and are born with it. This means we inherit spiritual death or separation from God. And you ladies don't think that you're left out of this death because the words 'all men' means mankind. You're included too, so listen close.

"Well, if we read on in Romans Five and go to verse nineteen, we find 'For as by one man's disobedience many were made sinners, so by the obedience of one shall many be made righteous.' Now you see here that not only our own sins makes us sinners, but we got it from Adam in our nature. So don't tell me you're not a sinner!" Now Leed was right with him on this, because he had figured this sinner thing out the other night. Preacher Bill never let up and went right on, "But where Adam made sinners, Jesus Christ, the One that the verse is talking about, made it so that many will be made righteous. Now if we back up a bit to Romans five, verse eight and read 'But God commendeth His love toward us, in that, while we were yet sinners, Christ died for us.' Look at that would ye, God knowed we was sinners and He sent His Son to die for us anyway!

"Now we know God loves us and He sent His Son to die for us. But how do we take advantage of this opportunity? Some people think you don't have to do nothing to be saved and that's wrong! In Hebrews chapter two and verse three, it says 'How shall we escape, if we neglect so great salvation;' so if you neglect something that means that you ain't doing something you're supposed to be doing. Now what do we do? Well, in Romans chapter five verses one and two we read 'Therefore being justified by faith, we have peace with God through our Lord Jesus Christ: By whom also we have access by faith into this grace wherein we stand, and rejoice in hope of the glory of God.' From that you can see this thing you have to do to be saved has something to do with faith because it says you're justified by faith and you have access to grace by faith.

"But let's think a minute here. What do you do with that faith, and what kind of faith is it? Well, if we go back in Acts, where people were a gettin' saved left and right, we can read in two places what this faith was used for. In Acts chapter nineteen, verse four we read 'Then said Paul, John verily baptized with the baptism of repentance, saying unto the people, that they should believe on Him which should come after him, that is, on Christ Jesus.' And then Acts chapter sixteen, verse thirty one 'And they said, Believe on the Lord Jesus Christ, and thou shalt be saved, and thy house.' Well it looks like they wouldn't just using a little simple faith, that was just good enough to use and say, 'Well I have enough faith to believe that Jesus Christ existed, that he was a real person.' No this faith they were using was saving faith because they used it to trust Jesus Christ for something. They believed in him for salvation, to save them from hell! Now that's real saving faith right there.

"In fact, we can't even muster up this saving faith on our own. It has to come from the Holy Sprit. Let's read over in Ephesians chapter two, verse eight 'For by grace are ye saved through faith; and that not of yourselves it is the gift of God.' So what this is telling us is that through God's grace we get the saving faith we need to believe in Jesus Christ as Savior so we can be saved. Now just think, this whole thing might look easy, and it is for us. You know why? Because this salvation that He wrought was so very difficult for Jesus Christ. He gave up His life on the cross so you could have the opportunity or grace for salvation, then God the Father raised Him from the dead and now gives you the saving faith you need for salvation. God has also kept you alive until this day so you could hear about this great salvation.

"So now I'm gonna' close with, 'don't neglect so great a salvation'. Let's all bow our heads, 'Father I ask that You would make this clear to everyone who has not accepted Your wonderful gift of salvation, so they will wait no longer because You have said, 'Today is the day of Salvation,' Amen.'

"Now for the invitation, James Hawk's son, Thomas James Hawk Jr., will sing 'Just as I Am'." Tommy Hawk walked up on the platform and got behind the podium while Preacher Bill stepped down to minister to anyone who came forward. Tommy started singing. Leed had listened closely during the whole service and had clearly understood for the first time God's plan to save people from Adam's as well as their own sin. He moved by Benji and out into the aisle and went down front and told Preacher Bill, "I've been away from God long enough; I want to get saved!" From back in the congregation Leed could hear a woman's sob and he knew it was his mom.

Preacher Bill asked, "Do I need to help you?"

Leed answered, "Please." As Tommy sang so beautifully, 'Just as I Am,' they bowed down at the altar together and Leed opened his heart to God, "Father, I know I'm a sinner and I repent the sins that I have committed against You. I thank You for the grace You have given me in Your Son; I accept the saving faith that You offer and I use it to believe in Your Son Jesus Christ as my personal Lord and Savior, Amen."

Preacher Bill was in no hurry to get up knowing that Leed was going back out into Satan's world and he needed to start his discipleship right now. Preacher Bill opened his Bible and showed Leed First John 5:13 'These things have I written unto you that believe on the name of the Son of God; that ye may know that ye have eternal life, and that ye may believe on the name of the Son of God.' Then Preacher Bill said, "When Satan, or worse, your own mind, tells you that what you have just done couldn't be true or it was too easy, remember we can trust the Word of God, but not Satan, who is the father of lies, and definitely not ourselves, because our thoughts run all over the place. Study in Romans every day next week, son, and you'll start growing spiritually.

Tommy was half way through the song again when Preacher Bill and Leed stood up. Tommy finished the verse he was on and went back to his seat and Preacher Bill announced that Leed was now a member of the family of God and everyone said a very loud "AMEN."

Leed went back to his seat where his dad stood, with tears in his eyes, and embraced his son. "You've made me so very thankful," Telford whispered. Afterwards, everyone gave him a hug, but the biggest hugs were from his mom and dad. This was a wonderful day for Leed and his family, and even Benji punched his arm in a gesture of approval.

That afternoon at home, and back at church that night, Telford and Linda could tell that Leed was a different person, relaxed, happy for the first time in a long time. They hugged each other and praised the Lord for His blessing.

This happiness carried over to work Monday and that night Leed went home and spent almost an hour in his Bible before he even opened an engineering book. Benji asked him in their room, "Why do you keep studying those books if you ain't going to Georgia Tech?"

Leed answered, "Well, I like studying them and I can always use the knowledge. It becomes part of my raisen'."

When he finished studying, it was late; but he felt good, so he went out on the porch and sat down in the swing. As he swayed gently back and forth, he noticed that the lightning bugs were out in force and were still lighting up well, even though it was long past dark. He smiled as he realized that they hadn't looked that beautiful since he was a boy out catching them in a quart fruit jar with holes poked in the lid. He stood up and walked down the steps and out into the night, looking up at the beautiful stars overhead. He marveled at how beautiful everything was now that he knew the Creator God who had made it all. Everything in the night brought joy to his heart: the chirr of the crickets, the whirling screech of a screech owl up on Crumley Mountain and the far away wail of a pack of fox dogs as they chased an ever-elusive fox, never to catch it for their master, but just for the joy and sound of the hunt. Later, he went to bed, content, with a smile on his face and in his heart.

The next day Leed was the same happy guy at work and when they got home the whole family was in the kitchen eating when they heard someone drive up out in the yard. Linda stood up and went to the window, "It's Jordan Laycock in his new pickup." Telford met Jordan at the front door where they talked for just a minute, and then Telford called out, "Ya'll come in here for a minute. We can finish supper after while."

Linda, Benji and Leed all got up and came into the front room with a little edge, not knowing what was going on.

Telford opened, "Jordan has something to tell us."

Jordan smiled and said, "I was down in Atlanta the other day and I went by and talked to the president of Georgia Power about a new way to find and keep good engineers at Georgia Power. What we've come up with is this: if we can find a good engineering candidate who is willing to sign an agreement that, number one, he will keep his grades above a B; number two, he will work each summer, while he is in school, for an hourly wage in a local office somewhere in the state where we need him; and, number three, he will agree to work for Georgia Power, after graduation at normal pay for two years for every one year of school that Georgia Power pays for, we may be able to help deserving young men get an education. During his years of required employment," he further explained, "the candidate is to pay back his school bill to Georgia Power without interest. With this program, we can help other promising young engineers who couldn't otherwise go to college."

Leed stood there with his mouth hanging open the whole time Jordan was talking. He was amazed at how good God is and how good a friend that Jordan had become. Jordan looked at him and said, "Well, what do you think, Leed? Would you like to go to Georgia Tech?" "Yes! Yes!" Leed shouted. And the whole family echoed his answer and went to hugging each other and laughing. Leed even hugged Jordan before he thought.

After everything settled down, Jordan said, "I went by Georgia Tech and got the papers to fill out so you could go ahead and register. You can get into Tech this fall. There is a small registration fee and you will also have to pay for all of your books and supplies at school. Can you handle that?"

"Sure," Telford said, "that we can handle."

18 CLEANSING THE MOUNTAIN

The next night after church, when Leed and Benji were in their room, Leed looked troubled so Benji asked, "You been happy the last few days, why are you sulled up like a big possum now fer?"

"Well," Leed answered, "I'm about to go off to school and leave everybody here. But there's one thing that I need to take care of before I go. Ronnie and Lonnie are still running that still and the 'hydro balance separator'. They have to be stopped before someone else gets killed."

"You're right," said Benji, "I'll help you and I think Tommy Hawk will too. We've got to destroy that 'hydro' thang."

Leed said, "OK then, it's our responsibility to take care of this once and for all. We'll need a plan; I think they have a still around the back of the mountain, somewhere down the river. We'll search around the mountain tomorrow and try to find it."

Thursday after work they slipped around the mountain and found the still. They were afraid to get too close, but they could see Ronnie stirring the mash and Lonnie gathering wood to fire the boiler, and they were close enough to hear them say they were going to make a run tomorrow.

They eased back quietly, went to Tommy Hawk's and told him their plan. They asked their dad for the day off to scoot board on Friday, as a cover for what they were really going to do: attack the still house. They planned to go at midday.

Tommy Hawk came over late the next morning and they went

out to the shed and got their scoot boards.

"To conserve our strength, I've borrowed grandpa's Model-T to haul us up the old logging road to the top of the mountain. When we get to the top we will go to the scoot boards. Now let's go," said Leed. They went over to grandpa's barn and cranked the Model-T, loaded up and puttered and bounced to the top of the mountain.

Leed laid out the plan of attack after they were parked. "We'll scoot right down the face of the mountain to the cliff, turn and go right down the spine of the steep ridge toward the river. They have the still house, which ain't nothing but some boards with a little tin over the top of it, settin' right on the left side of the ridge spine, up out of the branch. If we go down the left side of the spine to the laurel thicket and then jump across the ridge to the right side, we'll be on them before they know it. Then we can cross back over and surprise them."

"When we get there, Tommy Hawk, you scoot by first so you can draw Ronnie out of the still house with the gun. Be careful and jump right back over the ridge to the right as quick as possible to get out of rifle range in case Benji fails. Benji, you'll be next. Now you need to stay about thirty yards behind Tommy Hawk to give Ronnie time to come outside with the gun. When he does, try to scoot by and just grab the gun from him. If you can't, then just scoot into him and knock him a windin'. You just disarm or take out Ronnie and I'll be right behind you and I'll take care of Lonnie and then grab the 'hydro balance separator'." The whole time he'd been talking, he'd been drawing out the plan of attack with a broken limb, in the soft earth of the mountain top.

"When I have the 'hydro balance separator' everyone scoots into the thicket along the branch and down the hill toward the river to the lower trail. Then pick up your scoot board and run fer the house. When we get there we'll chop the 'hydro balance separator' into little pieces of copper the size of pennies."

"Now, does everyone understand what to do?" Leed asked.

Tommy Hawk gave his usual silent nod and Benji said, "There could be trouble after this if we succeed. We may have to go to war with Ronnie and Lonnie over this." Leed looked solemn and said, "Yeah, I know, but they're responsible for the deaths of two of our friends and we can't fail! So we better pray before we go." They all dropped to one knee and Leed prayed, "Father, there's evil on this mountain and we ask You to remove it and cleanse the mountain. We're going down there in harm's way and we ask You for protection and help." They each walked back to the T Model and got out their scoot boards, tucked them under their arms and walked with steady, straight, determined steps across the top of the mountain down to where it was steep enough to use the scoot boards. Then they rigged up and started sliding down the face of the mountain.

They were all zigging and zagging through the trees and Benji got out into the lead and Tommy Hawk tried to stay up with him. Leed was several yards behind and he knew with all of the adrenaline flowing, they were going too fast. He sped up and tried to catch up and as he did Tommy Hawk's board hooked a root and flipped him. He landed hard on his left shoulder and then rolled over a couple of more times. As Leed went by him he looked back for just an instant. When he looked forward, he was almost into a tree. He moved his body but still had to go down to keep from hitting the tree and when he did his scoot board hooked the tree and threw him hard down the hill where he piled up worse than Tommy had.

Leed sat up and shook his head to clear it and tried to get up, but he couldn't; his left leg and knee had hit the ground pretty hard and were hurting. He looked up the hill and there was Tommy Hawk, walking toward him holding his left arm up with his right hand and appeared to have a broken arm or collar bone. Leed got about half way up on his right knee and looked down the hill, and there was Benji stopped and looking back up at them. Leed waved for him to come back. The attack was off as far as he was concerned.

But Benji thought different. He gave his older brother a solemn look, shook his head 'no', then turned and jumped into his scoot board and started on down the face of the mountain. Leed, not believing that Benji would so readily go into the face of danger, hollered, "Benji stop, stop! You can't do it by yourself!" He turned to Tommy Hawk, who was standing just above him, looked up and just stared. Tommy Hawk said, "He will need help. We should pray." Tommy Hawk knelt by Leed, still holding his shoulder, and bowed his head and said, "Father, Benji really needs Your help. We ask that You would provide help for Benji as he continues this attack without us." Leed came right in and said, "Yes, Father, we ask

You to send Benji a helper to destroy this evil."

They kept praying as Benji, now out of sight, neared the cliff. Benji lined himself up to scoot right straight at the top edge of the cliff, then he would grab one of the ropes they had tied there so he could swing out over the cliff. He figured that the rope would swing him around and accelerate him so when he came back across the end of the rocks, he would head down the spine of the ridge at full speed.

Just as he went off the cliff, he grabbed the rope, but it was a bit more excitement than he had planned for. As he went out and started the arc, he gave out a yell that went up and down till he swung back around and hit the leaves again. It sounded ever so much like a Tarzan yell.

Lonnie was standing just out of the still house further down the mountain, when he heard the faint Tarzan yell. He looked real puzzled, then stepped back into the still house where Ronnie was catching the distilled white liquor in a jar as it came out of the 'hydro-balance-separator', and asked, "Does Tarzan live around here?" "No Tarzan don't live around here!" answered Ronnie, "now get back to work!" Lonnie mumbled something and starting capping the jars that had cooled down a little.

The swing had reaccelerated Benji after the slow-down in the small flat area above the cliff, and he was now going down the left side of the spine of the ridge just as Leed had planned. Benji dropped into a low stance and got a little more speed in anticipation of jumping over the ridge to set up his approach on the other side. His scoot board was making a swift, swishing sound as he came down that side of the spine.

It so happened at that very moment a local resident, with somewhat of a reputation, was out on an afternoon stroll, just walking along down the right side of the spine of the ridge, heading for the river. He had not a care in the world until suddenly he heard a swishing sound coming from the other side of the ridge. It alerted him and he took off running before this fast moving swishing thing could get him. Just as he got up to speed right along the right side of the spine, Benji crossed over at full speed and got a lot of altitude. As he came down, he landed right on the back of the high-speed local resident. As a result, an absolutely terrified Slewfoot ran even faster.

Benji and Slewfoot were heading in almost the same direction, at almost the same speed, when Benji jumped across the spine of the ridge and landed on his back, so he was able to stay up on Slewfoot's back for a few feet, balanced on his scoot board. But the flexing hulk of the gigantic, running bear quickly bounced him off as he crossed over to the left side of the ridge. Benji rolled out of it well, flipped off his scoot board, ran up on the spine where he looked down the left side of the ridge at Slewfoot heading straight for the still house, taking thirty feet a jump.

Lonnie looked out of the still house through an opening and saw Slewfoot heading straight at them. He said with a trembling voice, "Ronnie, there comes Slewfoot to get us for locking him in the trunk of mama's car! I'm skeered!" Then he ran out of the still house toward the branch.

As he did, Ronnie was already up and looking out the hole. Slewfoot was now almost to the still house, and not slowing down a bit. Ronnie dove out the other side of the shack and rolled out of the way, just as the big, black, furry, freight train hit the still house at full speed, knocking tin and planks fifteen feet in the air! As he tore on through, he busted the still and knocked mash barrels out both sides, splashing the white smelly mash all over the trees. When he came out the other side, he had a bunch of copper coils wrapped around him and the 'hydro balance separator' was held to his chest by the copper tubing. As he arrived at the river, he made a huge leap, landed on a big rock out in the river on his chest and crushed the 'hydro balance separator' into a flat piece of copper, that now came loose with the tubing. The current rolled the notorious apparatus off down the river into a deep hole never to be seen again.

Lonnie was already a half mile away and Ronnie wasn't far behind him, gaining fast, heading for the house. And Benji was still just standing on the spine of the ridge grinning and praising the Lord for the awesome sight he had just seen. Finally, he got his scoot board and headed back up the mountain. When he got to Leed and Tommy Hawk they were still praying and were really glad to see him. He was laughing and still shaking his head in amazement as he related the details. He finished with, "I guess Ronnie and Lonnie are at home by now and probably won't go back in the woods for awhile."

The three boys then praised the Lord. For He had taken care of everything even the concern that there would be war with Ronnie and Lonnie after this was over. Now, Ronnie and Lonnie didn't even know Benji, Leed and Tommy Hawk were involved. Leed got up and the pain wasn't as bad now and it looked to be just bruises, but it looked like Tommy Hawk's collar bone was for sure broken. They eased back up the mountain and got in the T Model and headed back home. They told their parents that Leed and Tommy Hawk had wrecked on their scoot boards, which they had, without giving any details of the true mission they were on.

Leed, Benji and Tommy sang at the top of their lungs in church Sunday because they were still full of praise for God and for what He had done on Friday. Leed was really enjoying going to church now and he was looking forward to going to Georgia Tech this fall. He was also enjoying his relationship with Jesus Christ now and that helped him to enjoy being himself more too.

On Tuesday Telford, Leed and Benji headed to town. On their way they saw Loge Rodgers walking up the road and Leed, who was on the passenger side, stuck his arm out the window and waved real big and hollered, "Hey Loge, how are you?" For the first time, Loge stopped, looked straight at Leed and just waved in a normal way, as his eyes followed them as they passed by and out of sight. Telford said, "Well son, I guess you just got too old Loge. I reckon he ain't never seen nobody as happy as you before."

They pulled on into town and while their dad was at the Standard station getting gas and oil, they walked down in front of the Rock house on Main Street in the center of Clayton and started talking to the old folks that gathered there and sat on the rock benches and talked. One old lady was asking Leed about him going to Georgia Tech and what he thought of it. He told her how excited he was. She said, "Well the Lord certainly is blessing you." Leed answered, "Yes, He is!"

As Leed and Benji headed back over toward the street, Cindy Lewis came down the sidewalk. She smiled shyly at Leed and said, "Hello Leed," and kept right on going. Leed's face broke out in a great big smile as he and Benji started back up to the Standard station. As they walked, Leed spontaneously broke out singing, "I wish I was an apple, a hanging on a tree, and every time that Cindy come by she could take a bite of me, get along home Cindy, Cindy, get along home Cindy, Cindy, get along home Cindy, Cindy, I'll marry you some day." Benji just shook his head and said, "Boy you got it bad!" Leed grabbed his arm and they took off racing to the pickup.

ABOUT THE AUTHOR

HOKE
SHIRLEY

Hoke Shirley was born in the mountains of north Georgia in 1953. He is a sixth generation Rabun Countian, who grew up listening to the stories that were told by his dad and other family members some true and some mountain fables intended to teach a lesson to the youn-guns'. Hoke beautifully weaves these tales into his own, in this heartwarming account of a mountain man raising two boys during hard times in rural Georgia.

Hoke Shirley and his wife Jackie live in the very mountains that are spoke of it this book. The Shirleys raised their three children in Rabun County and still reside there. Hoke enjoys spending time with his family, especially his six grandchildren, working in his church, hunting, fishing, and writing.

You are invited to contact Mr. Shirley for speaking engage-ments or to share your comments on his book or to purchase ad-ditional copies.

ORDERING INFORMATION
To obtain additional copies of this book please send $14.95 per copy plus $4.99 Shipping and Handling for a total of $19.94 per copy to:
Raisen'
P. O. Box 1512
Clayton, GA 30525
Or order online at www.laurelmountainpress.com

There is more to this story:

What happens to Leed as he ventures to the big city of Atlanta to get the education he wanted so badly? What evil will he have to address in Atlanta, or elsewhere? Does Danielle go to Georgia Tech? Will he graduate and become the engineer he is destined to be. . . The story continues in
Schoolin',
to be released in 2009

Who will win Leed's heart? Will he have a Georgia Tech education or will he have to take a public job? What happens at home and with the family? What great problems are waiting to be addressed out in the world?
Find these answers in the final book in this trilogy
by Hoke Shirley -
Workin' ,
to be released in 2010

RABUN COUNTY GEORGIA CROWN JEWEL OF THE SOUTHEAST

Rabun County Georgia is my mountain home. I praise God that he allowed me to grow up in such a beautiful place. Comprised of approx. 60% US Forest Service land, approx. 12% Georgia Power Company land and lakes and approx. 3% State Parks, Rabun County is a playground for an outdoorsman such as me.

Rabun County is the extreme northeastern county in Georgia. It is bordered on the North by the 35° parallel which is the North Carolina state line, on the East by the Chattooga River which is the South Carolina state line, on the South by Tallulah Gorge and a mountain ridge that forms just out of the gorge and runs all the way to the predominate Western boundary of Rabun County which is the Appalachian Trail.

DRAINAGE AND RIVERS:

Soon after this mountain ridge leaves Tallulah Gorge it becomes the Eastern Continental Divide which divides the Tallulah/Tugaloo/Savannah River Drainage which runs into the Atlantic Ocean from the Soque/Chattahoochee/Apalachicola River basin which runs into Apalachicola Bay in the Gulf of Mexico.

After the Eastern Continental Divide reaches the Appalachian Trail at the top of Young Lick Mountain it joins the Tennessee Valley Divide and follows the Appalachian Trail several miles north along the Rabun County line. The Eastern Continental Divide now separates the Hiawassee/Tennessee/Ohio/Mississippi River Drainage which runs into the Gulf of Mexico from the Tallulah/Tugaloo/Savannah River Drainage which runs into the Atlantic Ocean.

This point on the Appalachian Trail, the top of Young Lick Mountain, is a triple drainage point which is rare on this scale. It is the point where water separates to go to Savannah Georgia on the Atlantic Ocean and to New Orleans and Apalachicola Bay both on the Gulf of Mexico.

The Eastern Continental Divide runs north along the Appalachian Trail into North Carolina then leaves the Appalachian Trail and come back into Rabun County following the mountain tops down to where it crosses US Highway 441/23 in Mountain City in north central Rabun County. The Eastern Continental Divide crossing is noted on the highway with a sign that says Blue Ridge Divide. At this point the Eastern Continental Divide now separates the Little Tennessee/Tennessee/Ohio/Mississippi River Drainage which runs into the Gulf of Mexico from the Chattooga/Tugaloo/Savannah River Drainage which runs into the Atlantic Ocean. It then turns back into North Carolina and continues on to its end in Pennsylvania.

The Chattooga River is not only the state line between Georgia and South Carolina after it enters from North Carolina at Ellicott's Rock, but it is also a federally designated 'Wild and Scenic River'. It has a protected corridor along both sides and has many miles of hiking trails to see the great beauty of this mountain river. The river has up to class five rapids and is a challenge to the many rafters, kayakers and canoe paddlers that frequent the river.

The upper portion of the Chattooga River is a fisherman's paradise and has special regulations in some areas to enhance the fishing experience.

The Tallulah River enters Georgia in Towns County, runs through Tate City then shortly into Rabun County at Line Branch. This upper section of the Tallulah River is accessible from Tallulah River Road which turns left off of Persimmon Road about five miles up from US Highway 76. I consider the drive up Tallulah River Road along the upper section of the Tallulah River to be the most beautiful in the state of Georgia. This section of the river offers great fishing, intense beauty, boulders in the river as big as cabins, and is a photographer's as well as a fisherman's dream.

Below this section the Tallulah River levels out a little and forms Lake Burton, Seed Lake, Rabun Lake and Tallulah Falls Lake which offer great fishing, boating and other recreational opportunities. These lakes are some of the most beautiful in the world with the blue/green waters surrounded by the green mountains in the summertime.

Next the Tallulah River runs through the Tallulah Gorge before joining the Chattooga River in Tugaloo Lake to form the Tugaloo River. The Gorge is enclosed in the Tallulah Gorge State Park which has an interpretive center, campground, many hiking trails, a suspension bridge over the almost six hundred foot vertical drop. This is truly an awesome, almost scary place to visit.

On July 18, 1970, my cousin and I parked my 1955 Chevrolet, almost a mile north of Tallulah Falls and walked down US Highway 441, across the bridge and stood on the Highway Right-of-Way (we didn't have the money for the $10 ticket to get to a better location) to watch Karl Wallenda walk across the Gorge on a three inch cable. We were so far away that the only way we could tell that he was standing on his head for the troops in Vietnam was when the gold and red of his outfit inverted. He was wearing gold pants and a red shirt or vice-versa.

Another interesting thing about the Gorge is that my three brothers and I were told that if you drop a strike-anywhere match off of the US Highway 441 Bridge, that the friction of the air would ignite it before it hit the bottom. We doubted this so we went to the kitchen next to the wood cook stove and got a bunch of strike-anywhere matches and got our dad to take us to the Gorge in his 1941 Ford pickup for a test. As we dropped the matches they would sometime ignite but only from impact as they struck the dry rocks below. So to confirm the test after we arrived home (do not try this at home or in the gorge (would be considered littering) as this type of activity is reserved for crazy mountain boys who want to be engineers and alternative methods now exist) we took our BB guns and cocked them empty then stood them straight up and dropped one strike-anywhere match down the barrel and fired them into our concrete steps. Most of them would ignite. So we surmised from two independent tests that the impact was the ignition source, not friction.

Another note about the gorge is the great challenge it presents to the travel of wildlife. I spent eleven years driving to Toccoa Georgia working at a plant just below Toccoa. I would drive thirty miles one way and drop over 1,000 feet in altitude to my job. I took special notice of all the wildlife that was ran over along the road as I drove the sixty miles each day. One thing of very special interest was that of only three raccoons that I saw lying along the road during the eleven years, two of them were lying, ran over on the US 441 Bridge that crossed the Tallulah Gorge. The normal caution of the raccoons was put aside to take the easy two minute route over the bridge, to cross this huge cut in the earth, instead of the dangerous several hour climb down and back up the walls of the Gorge, in the few spots that this was even possible.

Many other wonderful trout streams are available in Rabun County for the fisherman's pleasure also.

With the extreme elevation variation of 3,804 feet available in Rabun County and the historically very high rainfall averages, Rabun County is home to many very beautiful waterfalls. Here is an alphabetical list of the more popular falls, most of which have a trail or road leading to them. Many smaller branch falls exist but can only be seen by hiking directly through the woods in very rough terrain. Ada-Hi Falls, Ammons Creek Falls, Angel Falls, Bad Branch Falls, Becky Branch Falls, Bull Sluice, Crow Creek Falls, Darnell Creek Falls, Denton Branch Falls, Dick's Creek Falls, Hemlock Falls, Holcomb Creek Falls, Hurricane Falls, Kilby Mill Falls, Ladore Falls, Martin Creek Falls, Minnehaha Falls, Mud Creek Falls, Panther Falls, Stonewall Falls, Sweet Sixteen Falls, Sylvan Lake Falls, Tempesta Falls and Upper Falls.

The naming of places you find on maps has always intrigued me as you find some places named after a person or family, such as Darnell Creek. This leads me to wonder who these people were. Other places are named for close by settlements, such as Tiger Mountain and that is easy to understand. Still other are related to natural features of the land such as Stone-pile Gap. The two most intriguing names in Rabun County come from the shores of Tugaloo Lake on the Georgia side up near where the Chattooga River runs into the lake. As the pioneers explored this area they came upon this rough area and named the first branch Bad Branch, soon they came to the next branch and named it Worse Branch. This is some rough country.

Of all the falls my favorite is Stonewall falls which is one mile directly behind my home. In 1985 when I built my home, all of the sweat equity that I invested in it wore me out, so to refresh myself I removed the top of my Bronco that summer (rain and shine). Also after working my ten hour job and almost to dark on the house I would go to Stonewall Falls and bathe and finish most days on the 'throne' getting a cold water massage.

MOUNTAINS AND TRAILS:

Rabun County has four of the ten highest mountains in the state of Georgia including the second highest, Rabun Bald at 4,696 feet above sea level and the third highest, Dicks Knob at 4,622 feet above sea level. Of the mountains in Rabun County eight are over 4,000 feet above sea level and if you count all tops, even those that are unnamed or are adjacent to other named mountains you find eighty that are over 3,000 feet above sea level. The lowest point in Rabun County is the bottom of Tallulah Gorge at the edge of Tugaloo Lake which is 892 feet above sea level. This gives Rabun

County an extreme elevation variation of 3,804 feet.

The mountains of special interest to me in Rabun County include Rabun Bald, Blackrock Mountain, Glassy Mountain, Young Lick, Dismal Knob, Tiger Mountain, Pinnacle Knob and Hellhole Mountain (don't go hunting there unless you have strong friends to drag your deer).

Rabun County in reality is one mountain range located in front of or behind another so the roads all wind up the steep valleys in between the mountains. To really enjoy the beauty of this area one of the many trails can be hiked to the many mountain tops that they traverse to get some awesome views of the surrounding mountains.

The many trails in Rabun County include the Appalachian Trail, Bartram Trail, Angel Falls Trail, Chattooga River Trail, Coleman River Trail, Hemlock Trail, Holcomb Creek Trail, Minnehaha Trail, Rabun Bald Trail, Raven Rock Trail, Sutton Hole Trail, Three Forks Trail, Warwoman Dell Nature Trail, Willis Knob Horse Trail and many other hiking, bike and ORV trails.

COOKIN' AND EATIN':

The mountain folks really love to cook and eat and they are really good at both. I love cooking the old timey way with a wood cook stove so when I built my house I provided a place for the wood range. I soon found out why my mom's house which is over one hundred years old has the kitchen as a wing out away from the house accessible only by going out onto the porch and then into the kitchen. Cooking in the house with a wood cook stove will definitely heat your house up in a hurry. Our wood range is reserved pretty much for special occasions to cook with my grandchildren who think it is a very special treat to cook with wood. A well installed wood range with all the support tools also makes a very attractive addition to a country home.

Cornbread, soup beans, biscuits, gravy, jelly and chocolate gravy are absolute mountain staples and with real hog lard for your grease you can get your cholesterol fix for a whole week in one meal. I long ago went to canola oil so I would not OD on hog fat. The mountain folks can really show their cooking prowess at big family get-to-gathers, church gatherings and other major mountain social events. Eating out at one of the many fine eating places in Rabun County is also a culinary delight.

Of all the eating out places I have ever gone to one is so far above all the others that I use it as the description of where I am from. When I travel and people ask where I am from I first say, "Rabun County Georgia," and many know where that is. If that doesn't work then I say, "Clayton Georgia," and a few more now know where I live. If these fail I say, "do you know where the Dillard House is," and most of the time their eyes light up and they say, "yes". The Dillard House specializes and excels in cooking the old timey way and they are famous for there wonderful dishes, great hospitality and beautiful facilities.

PEOPLE, CULTURE AND FOXFIRE:

Many intelligent and talented people live in the mountains. But because of the limited educational opportunities in the past many foreigners (defined as non mountain folks), not just limited to the educated elite, look down on mountain folks. This is a tragedy since it is predicated on ignorance. The fact that they are not acquainted with us, as a special people, and our culture, which is so important to us, leaves little room for understanding and proper admiration for our great contributions to society.

The Foxfire books which come from here in Rabun County have done a great service to help the world understand these wonderful people and their value. My grandfather Benny Eller was in one of the Foxfire magazines and is a good example of an uneducated but intelligent and talented mountain man. Benny could barely write but I consider him to be a very good engineer. Having worked with him many summers I know he could design and build many projects with the minimum of tools and time and he specialized in constructing the straightest fences around, which was an item of utmost pride. In fact after we would build a long straight fence he would site back down the fence row and state, "Now that's as straight as an arrie' (for arrow)".

Benny also supplied several of the stories for this book. The running from the revenuer's scene was experienced by him and his dog chasing his brother as they ran from the revenuers above Plum Orchard Creek around Chestnut Mountain. The turkeys in the tree and the honey and bee larvae were experienced by his father whom he call pow-paw (written the way he pronounced it).

Foxfire also maintains a complete settlement of relocated log homes, cabins, barns and corn cribs in Mountain City that can be toured for a nominal fee. My good friend Rob Murray is the curator and knows the history of all the buildings because he helped move most of them. A tour led by Rob is very informative.

Foxfire also helps sustain one of my favorite things about the mountain culture, and that is Bluegrass Music. The Foxfire Boys have been together since they were in Foxfire high school classes back in the early eighties and are still making great Bluegrass Music. They are all good friends of mine and have been to my house and practiced much to my delight. Two of the Foxfire Boys now have a music shop and are teaching their music to the next generation.

The Foxfire Boys as well as many other Bluegrass and Gospel groups in Rabun County are tireless in their efforts to help those who have needs. Fund Raisers for those in need and for certain groups and organizations are very common in the mountains and these bands offer their services free on a regular basis to help. They do not consider the cost of time, travel or equipment out of their own pockets but just say yes and show up to help.

One of the greatest Bluegrass shows each year is at the Satolah Fire House located at 2396 Highway 28 North in Satolah Georgia. Each year, on the first day of trout season in Georgia, many anglers are drawn to the many trout streams in the area. The Satolah Volunteer Fire Department has a big Barbeque and Bluegrass show to raise money for equipment. The Foxfire Boys have donated their time for many years and one or more other bands also show up for what I consider to be the highlight of the Bluegrass year. George Reynolds formerly the Foxfire music and folklore teacher at Rabun County High School said that the Satolah crowd was the most sophisticated Bluegrass crowd in the world. He qualified his statement by noting the reason was because a large percentage of the people attending played Bluegrass Music themselves.

Rabun County has many churches and many fine pastors who are teaching their flocks about the need to prepare now for their coming stint in eternity. I thank them for their faithfulness in proclaiming God's Word as truth.

by HOKE SHIRLEY